Family Tree

Mary
(b. 1813)

Henry Quiner
(1807–1844)

CAROLINE
(1839–1924)

Eliza
(1842–1931)

Thomas
(1844–1903)

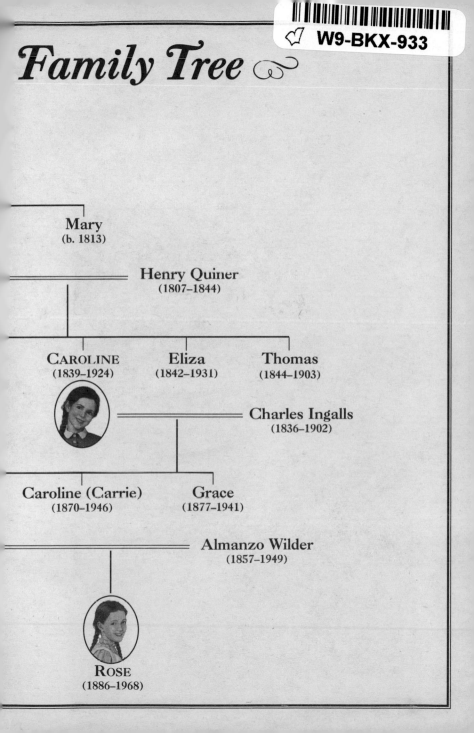

Charles Ingalls
(1836–1902)

Caroline (Carrie)
(1870–1946)

Grace
(1877–1941)

Almanzo Wilder
(1857–1949)

ROSE
(1886–1968)

Little Town
at the
Crossroads

Maria D. Wilkes

Illustrations by Dan Andreasen

HarperTrophy ®
A Division of HarperCollins*Publishers*

To my mother and father,
whose loving home I
return to again and again,
in thought, in spirit, and in heart.

Harper Trophy®, ☕®, Little House®, and The Caroline Years™
are trademarks of HarperCollins Publishers Inc.

Little Town at the Crossroads
Text copyright © 1997 by HarperCollins Publishers Inc.
Illustrations © 1997 by Dan Andreasen
Printed in the United States of America. For information address
HarperCollins Children's Books, a division of HarperCollins Publishers,
10 East 53rd Street, New York, NY 10022.
http://www.harperchildrens.com

Library of Congress Cataloging-in-Publication Data
Wilkes, Maria D.
    Little town at the crossroads / Maria D. Wilkes ; illustrations by Dan
Andreasen.
    p.   cm.
    Summary: Young Caroline Quiner, who would grow up to become
Laura Ingalls Wilder's mother, and her family have new adventures as
the frontier outpost of Brookfield, Wisconsin, grows into a bustling town.
    ISBN 0-06-440651-2 (pbk.) — ISBN 0-06-026995-2.
    ISBN 0-06-026996-0(lib. bdg.)
    1. Ingalls, Caroline Lake Quiner—Juvenile fiction. [1.Ingalls,
Caroline Lake Quiner—Fiction.   2. Wilder, Laura Ingalls, 1867–1957—
Family—Fiction.   3. Frontier and pioneer life—Wisconsin—Fiction.
4. Wisconsin—Fiction.   5. Family life—Wisconsin—Fiction.]
I. Andreasen, Dan, ill.   II. Title.
PZ7.W648389Lk   1997   96-48096
[Fic]—dc21   CIP
                                                                  AC

❖
First Harper Trophy edition, 1997.

Author's Note

Before Laura Ingalls Wilder ever penned the Little House books, she wrote to her aunt Martha Quiner Carpenter, asking her to "tell the story of those days" when she and Laura's mother, Caroline, were growing up in Brookfield, Wisconsin. Aunt Martha sent Laura a series of letters that were filled with family reminiscences and vividly described the Quiners' life back in the 1800s. These letters have served as the basis for LITTLE HOUSE IN BROOKFIELD *and* LITTLE TOWN AT THE CROSS-ROADS, *the first books in a series of stories about Caroline Quiner, who married Charles Ingalls and became Laura's beloved Ma.*

The Caroline Quiner Ingalls whom I've come to know through Aunt Martha's letters, personal accounts, and my own research is, I was surprised and delighted to discover, even more animated, engaging, and outspoken than the fictional Caroline whom millions of readers have grown to know and love. I have presented the most realistic account possible of Caroline Quiner's life in LITTLE TOWN

AT THE CROSSROADS, *while still remaining true to the familiar depiction of Ma in the Little House books. I would like to thank everyone who contributed historical and biographical information and who directed me toward significant original sources, diaries, and documents, especially William Anderson, Martin Perkins, Lorraine Schenian, Terry Biwer Becker, Cindy Arbiture, Bob Costello, and Professor Rodney O. Davis.*

—M.D.W.

Contents

Little Town
at the
Crossroads

Fifes and Flags

"Wait for me, Caroline! I can't walk fast as you!"

Caroline squeezed her little sister's hot, sticky hand and pulled her along. "If we don't hurry, Eliza, we're going to miss everything!"

"I can't go any faster!" four-year-old Eliza whimpered.

"Caroline Lake Quiner," Mother said, "slow down! The Glorious Fourth has barely begun. We'll not miss a moment of the speeches and parade, I daresay, no matter how slowly we walk."

1

"But Mother, Anna's waiting in town," Caroline protested as she dropped Eliza's hand and slowed her steps. "Oh, why do I *always* have to mind Eliza? She walks so slow!"

"At least you don't have to watch *him*!" Martha chimed in as Thomas wrenched his pudgy fingers out of her hand and scurried off in a fit of giggles. Braids flying behind her, Martha hurried after her little brother, grabbed him by one brown suspender, and set him back on course. "By the time he gets all the way to town, it will be time to go back home!" she added crossly.

Swinging a round straw basket in a wide arc, Henry looked over his shoulder and grinned at Martha. "Well, that would mean you'd miss seeing Charlie! Horrors, Miss Martha!"

"Oh you just *hush*, Henry Quiner!" Martha shot back, her dark brown eyes flashing at her brother. Caroline had seen awful looks like this on her older sister's face before, and she hoped that Martha would hold her tongue, no matter how much Henry teased her. Today was the Fourth of July, and Caroline didn't want anything to spoil their celebration.

Brookfield was perfectly suited to greet the Glorious Fourth. The bright summer sun inched its way above silvery snips of clouds that hemmed the deep blue sky. Carefree breezes frolicked about, rousing forests of maple leaves and rippling fields of tall grass and wildflowers. White tangles of oxeye daisies, morning glories, and Queen Anne's lace draped the edges of the roads and the meadows beyond the frame houses like delicate drifts of snow. Every road bustled with townsfolk dressed in their Sunday best, heading to the crossroads of town to celebrate Independence Day.

"That's quite enough," Mother said calmly as Henry opened his mouth to tease Martha again. "Caroline and Martha, I need you to keep hold of Eliza and Thomas until we arrive in town and find a place to settle. As for you, Henry-O, watch the way you hold that basket. Swing it any higher, for goodness' sakes, and all the food will tumble right out! I can only hope that you haven't bruised the fruit already."

"I could swap baskets with him," Joseph offered. "I'm only carrying linens in mine and they can't get bruised, no matter how high Henry swings them."

"You needn't worry, Joseph." Grandma smiled knowingly at her oldest grandson. Nodding toward the basket rocking slowly in the crook of her arm, she confided, "I moved all the fruit in here before we left the house."

Zzzsss, pop! Zzzsss, bang!

Grabbing Eliza, Caroline dashed to the side of the road as three sizzling firecrackers wriggled past and popped with a quick flip and tumble on the bumpy road ahead.

"No need to practice your jig 'fore tonight, little Brownbraid." Henry laughed out loud. "Those firecrackers won't hurt anybody."

"All the same, Caroline and Eliza, walk along the edge of the road," Mother cautioned. "You too, Martha. One never knows where a firecracker might explode today." Glancing over at a noisy group of boys snaking their way through the crowd, she shook her head. "Those boys ought to know better."

"Well, amen for slowing down a minute, Charlotte! We've been following you a good while, but Sarah wouldn't let me holler 'cross the road to stop you. I thought we'd never catch you."

"Good morning, Benjamin! Good morning, Sarah!" Mother turned to greet her friends the moment she heard Mr. Carpenter's cheerful, husky voice. Mr. Carpenter was dressed in his finest Sunday suit. A carefully trimmed brown beard covered his cheeks and chin, and unlike most of the other men walking to town, he was holding his hat instead of wearing it. His thick brown hair was neatly combed and smoothed behind his ears, and it hung straight down to the tip of his shoulders.

"Can't recollect a prettier day for the Glorious Fourth. How 'bout you, little Brownbraid?" Mr. Carpenter asked.

"No, sir," Caroline answered honestly. She was only six years old, and she couldn't remember many Fourth of Julys. All she recalled was the cheering and music and noise she'd heard coming from town.

"Mr. Ben! Mr. Ben!" Eliza greeted him, her arms raised for a hug.

"Eliza! Eliza!" Mr. Carpenter laughed, and set his big basket on the dusty road. Pulling Eliza into his arms, he swung her, feet first, toward the sky.

"Benjamin Carpenter, watch how you handle that young lady!" Mrs. Carpenter admonished.

"Forgive me, Sarah. If I had me a girl, I'd know better," Mr. Carpenter joked. Gently he placed Eliza back on her feet and turned to greet Henry and Joseph.

"Hello, girls." Mrs. Carpenter beamed at Caroline, Eliza, and Martha. "You all look very pretty today."

"Thank you, ma'am," Caroline replied bashfully. Standing so close to Mrs. Carpenter, she couldn't help thinking that her own yellow church dress looked anything but pretty. Mrs. Carpenter's long-sleeved dress hugged her waist and ballooned out into a wide, round skirt that swayed from side to side as she walked. Wide tan-and-blue stripes fell from neckline to hem, each column embroidered with a velvety floral brocade. A fancy scarf flowed in a lacy arch over Mrs. Carpenter's head down to the middle of her sleeves, shading her face, hair, and shoulders from the bright sun. Caroline looked up at Mother's simple black dress and silently wished that Mother could wear beautiful dresses and scarves like Mrs. Carpenter's, instead of having to work so hard making such fine dresses for other ladies in Brookfield.

"Darned if the whole town's not come out to celebrate the Glorious Fourth! What say we hurry along before we get lost in this crowd?" Mr. Carpenter suggested.

"We'll follow you, Benjamin," Mother agreed.

Boom! Boom!

The maple leaves shook and the wildflowers trembled as a series of ear-splitting blasts pierced the air. Eliza shrieked and clutched Caroline's fingers so tightly that Caroline had to pull her hand away. "What was that?" Eliza cried.

Heart pounding, Caroline shook her stinging fingers. "It's a Fourth of July sound, Eliza. I do remember that!"

"It's just a blast of gunpowder, little one," Mr. Carpenter explained. "Sure enough, old Stam's exploding it under his anvil. I expect we'll be hearing those blasts all day. Wouldn't be Independence Day without them!"

"It means we're missing everything, Eliza!" Caroline cried. "Let's go!"

Caroline was in such a hurry to get to the crossroads of town that she didn't pay any more attention to the conversation between Mother and the Carpenters. It wasn't until Henry blurted out, "Pardon me, Mr. Ben! Where's Charlie?" that Caroline slowed down long enough to glance sideways at Martha. She watched as her older sister gazed down at her dusty shoes and her cheeks turned from pink to red.

"Sarah and I were hoping we could all picnic together," Mr. Carpenter replied. "So I told Charlie to run ahead and find a shaded bit of meadow that's big enough for all of us.

I just hope he got here early enough to stake our claim!"

"We'd be happy to join you," Mother said as Henry winked at Martha. "Joseph, Henry-O, run on ahead and find Charlie. The three of you together will certainly be able to save a good-sized spot for our picnic."

"Yes, ma'am!" the boys called out.

Martha looked at Caroline as her brothers disappeared down the crowded road. Her eyes were sparkling, and a soft blush remained in her cheeks. Her hair was tightly braided and smoothed beneath her bonnet, and her blue church dress flowed down her long, slender frame. Martha looked prettier than ever. Caroline was glad that Henry had run on ahead and taken all his teasing with him.

The road grew even more crowded and noisy as the Quiners and Carpenters neared the crossroads of town, and the joyful strains of a fiddle suddenly skipped along on the breeze. Caroline whirled around to find a whole group of people nodding their heads and clapping as a fiddler fiddled and two lanky boys, shirt-sleeves pushed up to their elbows and fists clenched at their waists, hopped and twirled and kicked their heels together in the air.

"Seventy years! I stand here today, friends, to remind you it's been seventy years!"

A deep voice shouting urgently above the fiddle startled Caroline, and she stood on her tiptoes and excitedly searched the crowd until she located the speaker. A stocky man with twirly whiskers had climbed onto a wide tree stump on the side of the road. He wore a tall black hat, striped gray-and-black trousers, and a black coat that angled down the back of his legs like two pointed tails. Standing a head above the crowd, the man waved his arms and shook his fists as townsfolk gathered around him and listened to every stirring word he spoke.

"This great country of ours is no grayer than my grandfather would have been had he not been murdered by the British scoundrels who thought they could keep us from our freedom and our great land! Well, I say, Never! Never!"

"Never!" the crowd shouted back.

"To any man, any country, that tries to drive us from our land, I say you will never succeed! Never!" the man cried. "The greatest country on earth, our America, and we'll fight to keep it free till it's seven *hundred* and seventy years old. And then some!"

"Yes, sir! Yes, sir! Free! Free! Free!" the crowd answered, swinging their fists toward the speaker.

Caroline felt a hand cradling her elbow and looked up into Mother's smiling green eyes. "Makes you want to shout right along, doesn't it?" Mother asked.

Caroline nodded, the man's words echoing in her ears. Mother was right. Caroline felt like shouting and raising her fists too, but young ladies never shouted if they could help it. She remained quiet, but inside she couldn't help hollering *Free! Free! Free!*

"Let's find your brothers," Mother said.

The very moment they reached the center of town, Mr. Carpenter spotted the boys. "They're over there, Charlotte," he said, gesturing past a loud, crowded tavern. "See? In that field just past Bebber's place. Charlie and Henry are waving their arms so fast and furious, they're likely to go spinning off to Prairieville if we don't hurry up and join them!"

Mother turned to Caroline and Martha. "Eliza and Thomas can come along with Grandma and me now, so you can run on ahead and find Anna," she said. "You may bring her back for dinner if you like."

"We could help carry the baskets to the picnic spot, Mother, and then go look for Anna," Martha offered.

Caroline looked at Martha in surprise. Martha rarely wanted to do anything but play, but now she was offering to stay and help Mother instead of hurrying off to join the celebration in town. Caroline wanted to shout, "No!" but she held her tongue when she noticed that Mother was also looking at Martha in surprise. "Thank you, Martha, but we can handle all the baskets just fine. Run along now."

Once Caroline and Martha were alone, Martha was suddenly in a bigger hurry than

Caroline. "Let's find Anna fast," she called out above all the noise. "Then we can go back and help Mother set out dinner."

No matter how much she liked helping Mother, Caroline planned to spend every last minute before dinner in the midst of the festivities. But she didn't tell Martha. Instead, she declared, "I bet Anna's still at the shop with her father," took her sister's hand, and started off down the busy road.

All around Caroline and Martha, people chattered and laughed and greeted their neighbors with warm handshakes and hugs. Young children clung to their mothers' skirts, while their older brothers tossed firecrackers and gobbled up handfuls of popcorn, and their older sisters swung on tree swings and danced about the square. In front of every building, a cheery flag waved its stars and stripes in celebration.

Caroline and Martha wove their way in and out among the townsfolk as they passed the tavern and the blacksmith's shop. As they slowly approached the general store, Caroline noticed that dozens of flags billowed above the heads of a crowd of people who stood facing the storekeeper's stoop. No one spoke except for a few mothers and fathers, who shushed their little ones and quietly told them to stand at attention.

". . . to secure these rights, governments are instituted among men, deriving their just powers from the consent of the governed; that whenever any form of government becomes destructive of these ends, it is the right of the people to alter or to abolish it, and to institute a new government, laying its foundations on such principles and organizing its powers in such form, as to them shall seem most likely to effect their safety and happiness. . . ."

The words sounded familiar to Caroline, and she knew that if a whole crowd of people stood silently listening to them, they must be very important, so she stopped and listened too. Did the voice, so clear and urgent above the crowd, belong to the same man who had been standing on a tree stump, shaking his fist and shouting "Free!"? Caroline stood as high as she could on her tiptoes and tried to look past the people who were blocking her view. But the crowd was too big, and all she could see were suit coats, hats, bonnets, and a few small parasols that bobbed color-fully above the crowd.

"Who do you suppose he is?" a lady in front of Caroline asked the man beside her.

"One of them politicians, for certain," the man answered. "Fancies himself governor should Wisconsin become a state."

"Let's go," Martha whispered, tugging lightly on Caroline's sleeve. "The sooner we find Anna, the sooner we can go back to help Mother."

"Shouldn't we stay and listen, Martha?" Caroline whispered back.

"He's just reading from the Declaration of Independence. It's the same thing Teacher reads us in school," Martha answered. "Today's not a school day, so we don't have to stand and listen. Let's go find Anna."

Caroline now remembered Miss Morgan

reciting the very same text in the schoolhouse. She insisted that every one of her students read it often enough to memorize each important word. As she slowly followed Martha away from the crowd, Caroline decided that she would learn that declaration by heart, as soon as she could read all those big words.

After hurrying past the shoemaker's shop and Hulsey's stable, Caroline and Martha finally arrived in front of the wheelwright's workshop.

"Hello, Anna!" Caroline called out to her friend as she peered inside the small building that Anna's father shared with the wagon maker. During the day, Joseph Short built cabinets and furniture in the shop. At night, he and Anna lived in the two rooms upstairs.

Anna's brown curls bounced about as she waved to Caroline and Martha. "Come! You must see what Papa is making!"

Stepping out of the bright sunlight into the dim shop, Caroline and Martha walked carefully around piles of wood, cabinets, tables, and chairs toward the back of the shop. Anna was leaning over her father's workbench as he whittled away at a small piece of wood.

"Look! Papa's making me a fife!" Anna said exuberantly.

"Mornin', Miss Caroline, Miss Martha," Anna's father greeted them in his heavy Scottish burr.

"Good morning, sir," Caroline and Martha answered politely.

Mr. Short looked up from his work, and Caroline thought for a moment that she was looking right at Anna's face, only it was much bigger and rounder. "Wish I'd had time to whittle another for you girls," he said. "Anna tells me you are so nice to her. But see? Time flies like the wind and I barely finished this." His voice trailed off as he pushed a handful of dark curls out of his eyes and glanced over at his daughter. "Be kind and share with your friends, eh darlin' Anna?"

"Of course, Papa," Anna replied. "Is it finished yet?"

"Try." Mr. Short handed Anna the fife and watched as she lifted it to her lips.

Anna's cheeks grew even more round and pink as she blew over the tiny holes of the instrument as hard as she could. High-pitched squeaks and squeals skirted from one side of the shop to the other.

"It's perfect!" Caroline clapped.

"Blow softer, Anna," Mr. Short suggested. "The sound will be much prettier."

"Yes, Papa," Anna replied happily.

"We must go. I hear the parade." Mr. Short smiled.

Leading the girls back through the front room, he stood beside the door as they stepped into the brilliant sunshine. Caroline caught her breath as a giant flag marched toward them, a swaying wave of red, white, and blue pointing up toward the heavens. A long line of men marched close behind, their trumpets and bugles blasting merrily. Still others followed, tapping, snapping, and booming their drums in response to the bugles' triumphant song.

"There are Henry and Joseph and Charlie!" Martha cried. "There, with the drummers!"

"The fifes and flutes are coming next, Anna. I hear them," Mr. Short said. He pointed toward the end of the parade, where another group of men, blowing a lilting, joyous melody, were surrounded by children of all sizes, who marched and skipped along. "Go now! You girls should march too."

"I'm going with Henry and Joseph, Caroline," Martha decided. "You stay with Anna, and we'll meet at the end of the parade."

Martha ran off to join her brothers before Caroline even had a chance to answer. At the very same moment, Anna reached for Caroline's hand, and together they dashed across the dusty road to join the parade.

Caroline and Anna marched through town, music blaring and flags waving all around them. As they passed the cobbler's shop, the trumpets and bugles, the drums and flutes and fifes, were suddenly still. The crowds that surrounded the parade on both sides of the road waved and cheered. When the instruments burst into song again, they played their perfect harmony joyfully, and all the beaming townsfolk sang the stirring melody:

> *"Hail! Columbia, happy land!*
> *Hail! Ye heroes, heav'n-born band!*
> *Who fought and bled in Freedom's cause,*
> *Let independence be our boast*
> *Ever mindful what it cost*
> *Ever grateful for the prize*
> *Let its altar reach the skies."*

Caroline didn't know every word to the glorious song, but she hummed along as best she could. The parade finally passed the crossroads of town, and Caroline saw Mother, Grandma, and the Carpenters on the side of the road, waving as they sang the final refrain:

> *"Firm, united, let us be,*
> *Rallying round our liberty;*
> *As a band of brothers join'd,*
> *Peace and safety we shall find."*

Parades and picnics, speeches and songs, fifes and flags! Caroline thought that no other day could be as exciting as Independence Day. As the parade ended and she and Anna hurried off to find Martha and the boys, Caroline decided she was very, very glad to be independent and free. If only they could celebrate their freedom more than one day a year!

Spelling Bee

For days following the Glorious Fourth, Caroline marched around the frame house, holding an imaginary fife to her lips and humming "Yankee Doodle." She marched while she pushed chairs to the table before every meal, she marched as she carried clean, dry dishes back to the dish dresser, she marched while she swept up the bedroom. She marched swiftly past Joseph and Henry splitting logs by the woodpile, more intent on staying in step than in dodging the stray chunks of wood spinning through the brightening skies. She marched as she tossed handfuls of oats and corn to the hens scratching and pecking at the dirt around her feet. She marched to school. She marched home. And when she wasn't marching, she and Anna were busy trying to coax a stirring melody out of Anna's fife.

One morning, Caroline was marching through a grassy meadow on her way to the schoolhouse when Martha interrupted her thoughts of parades, flags, and fifes.

"Sure hope you memorized the spelling words Teacher gave you for today," Martha said.

"Course I did," Caroline answered in time to her steps. "Same as every week."

"Good thing, 'cause Teacher's almost sure to pick you for the spelling bee today."

Martha's words halted Caroline's bare feet in mid march. "Why should she pick me?" she asked anxiously.

"Because it's been at least six weeks since school started, and 'most every student has already taken a turn. I was in one spelling bee, and Anna was too. But Miss Morgan's never once picked you. I'm almost certain she'll call you today."

Caroline's thoughts quickly turned to her page of spelling words. "We have to hurry, Martha, so I can study my words one more time before Teacher begins lessons."

Caroline sped across the meadow so quickly that she was inside the schoolhouse before anyone else. Slipping into her bench, she repeated her spellings over and over to herself while the sunny room filled with students. Slowly the chattering died down and Miss Morgan began lessons. Caroline never once looked up from her page of words until she heard Miss Morgan say, "Caroline Quiner, please come to the front of the room. I'd like you to represent the first primer students today."

Heart pounding, Caroline glanced at Martha, who was squeezed in tightly beside her on the crowded bench.

"Just keep thinking hard as you can up there," Martha whispered in her ear. "You know all the words. And try to forget that everybody's looking at you."

Caroline stood up and hastily smoothed her faded red dress over her petticoats. She smiled thinly at Anna and slowly made her way to the front of the room.

As she passed the eight rows of benches packed with girls of all ages and sizes and dotted with a handful of the youngest boys from town, Caroline wished that her stomach would stop flip-flopping. She had studied her page of spelling words for a whole week and had recited them to Mother and Grandma every day. She knew each word by heart, but she was still afraid that she'd forget all her spellings the moment she opened her mouth to recite them in front of the whole class.

Nearing the front of the room, Caroline also began wishing that she had worn her other dress. It, too, was a hand-me-down from Martha, but it wasn't nearly so faded as the red dress Caroline was wearing. Mother had replaced her collar and added a long sash that tied in a bow at the back. But the red dress was so worn, the tiny white dots printed all over it had practically disappeared into the fabric, and the once-cheerful red color had become a tired pink.

"Please stand with the other students on my right, Caroline," Miss Morgan directed, nodding to the girls beside her. Caroline took her place in line as Miss Morgan looked up and down the rows of benches, searching the room for another first-year student. "Elsa, please come to the front of the room," she finally said.

Standing on her tiptoes, Caroline peered at the back of the room. Elsa Schmidt was seated on the edge of the last bench, her shoulders slumped, her head bowed, and her thick brown hair hanging over her eyes. She didn't look up or move until Miss Morgan called her name again.

"Elsa Schmidt?" Miss Morgan repeated loudly and clearly. Elsa's head jerked up. Beneath her bangs, Elsa's brown eyes looked surprised and uncertain, as though she had heard her name but hoped she was mistaken.

"Please come to the front of the room, Elsa. It is your turn to participate in the spelling bee," Miss Morgan said crisply.

Elsa swallowed hard, looking frightened. A young boy with a straggly mop of curls and dirt-smudged cheeks seated beside Elsa nudged her sideways with his knee. Almost falling off the edge of the bench, Elsa quickly stood up and scuffled to the front of the room, dragging her bare feet across the wooden floorboards as if she dreaded every step.

As Elsa took her place opposite Caroline in the other line of spellers, Caroline didn't know whether to be relieved or worried. Elsa had lived in Brookfield for only a month, and she had started school two weeks later than everyone else. Twice, Caroline, Martha, and Anna had asked Elsa to play with them at recess, but both times Elsa had shaken her head and run off without a word. Caroline often spotted the strange girl sitting alone in the meadow beyond the schoolhouse, weaving wildflowers and grass into braided ropes that she later wore as necklaces. Soon after the Fourth of July, Caroline had seen Elsa with her mother and father at the general store. Elsa had looked away the moment Caroline waved to her. Caroline didn't have any idea how good a speller Elsa Schmidt was, but she had no doubt that Elsa was the most unfriendly girl she had ever met.

"All right, students," Miss Morgan said, "I will give each challenger three words. If you spell a word correctly, you will receive one point. If you do not spell it correctly, I will ask your counterpart on the opposing team to spell the same word. Whichever team first spells the word correctly will be awarded the point. As always, the team with the most points at the end of the spelling bee wins." Miss Morgan smiled at the students who stood nervously waiting to recite their spellings. "Are you ready, scholars?"

"Yes, ma'am," ten voices answered in unison.

"We'll begin with the youngest students today. Caroline, you will go first."

Caroline's heart began pounding so loud, she

was certain the first row of students could hear it. Closing her eyes, she concentrated as hard as she could on Miss Morgan's firm but gentle voice.

"The first word is 'mop,' Caroline."

Caroline took a deep breath and, her eyelids still tightly closed, answered in her surest voice, "Mop. M-O-P. Mop."

"That is correct, Caroline. One point for your team," Miss Morgan said. She reached for the slate pencil and scratched a vertical line on one side of the slate.

As Miss Morgan recorded the point, Caroline opened her eyes. Rows of faces were staring intently up at her from the packed benches in the schoolroom. Martha and Anna were sitting up as straight as they could, smiling over all the braided heads in front of them. Martha winked proudly.

"Elsa," Miss Morgan continued, "your word is 'fan.'"

Caroline looked over at the opposite team of spellers and waited for Elsa to begin. Elsa was scrunching the sides of her yellow cotton dress between her fists so tightly, Caroline could see her knuckles turning white. Without lifting her head, Elsa quietly answered, "F-A-N."

"Head up please, Elsa," Miss Morgan said patiently. "I'd like all the students in the classroom to hear your spelling."

The room was silent as Elsa stood stock-still, staring at a plump robin perched on the open windowsill beside her. A tall, freckled girl standing beside Elsa finally squeezed her arm, and Elsa immediately looked back at the schoolteacher.

"Repeat your spelling please, Elsa," Miss Morgan said again.

Clearing her throat quietly, Elsa slowly intoned, "F-A-N."

"Correct." Miss Morgan smiled, and scratched a line on the opposite side of her slate.

While the rest of the students in the spelling bee took their turns, Caroline watched Elsa. She wondered what was wrong with her. It was not very nice to refuse to speak to another student, but Caroline couldn't even imagine ignoring a schoolteacher's request. What if

Miss Morgan got so mad she rapped Elsa's knuckles, as she had done last week when one of the boys sassed her? He had burst into tears, and the whole scene had made Caroline miserable. As rude as Elsa had been to her and Martha and Anna, Caroline hoped she would start paying attention so she wouldn't get a caning too.

"We're ready to begin the next round," Miss Morgan was suddenly saying. "Caroline, your word is 'jam.'"

Caroline was too startled to be nervous. "Jam. J-A-M. Jam," she answered, speaking every letter as clearly as she could.

"Very good, Caroline," Miss Morgan said, and recorded another point for Caroline's team.

The very moment Miss Morgan turned to address the opposing team, the tall girl standing beside Elsa tugged on Elsa's sleeve. Lifting her head, Elsa peered through her bangs and listened carefully.

"Your word is 'sun,' Elsa, as in 'The sun is shining brightly today.'"

"S . . ." Elsa began, and hesitated for a moment.

"Continue, please," Miss Morgan urged.

"S . . ." Elsa paused again. "U," she said slowly. "N."

"That is correct, Elsa," Miss Morgan said. "Good for you."

Listening closely, Caroline didn't know whether to be pleased or angry. She was paying attention to Miss Morgan and spelling all her words quickly and correctly. But Elsa was watching the bird on the windowsill more than she was listening to the teacher, and practically had to force the letters from her lips when called upon. Elsa didn't even follow the spelling-bee rules. She recited letters without stating the word before she spelled it, yet Miss Morgan waited patiently for her answers and praised her responses. It didn't make any sense. Caroline looked over at Anna, who raised her eyebrows and looked as though she might burst into a fit of giggles. As quickly as she could, Caroline looked away from her friend and bit her bottom lip so she wouldn't start giggling too. Anna must be as confused as she was, she thought.

The remaining spellers on each team finished their words, and in no time at all Miss Morgan turned back to Caroline for the final round. Caroline knew that her last word would be the most difficult to spell, so she held her breath and waited for Miss Morgan to speak.

"Your final word is 'nest,' Caroline."

All the fear that had been churning inside disappeared when Caroline heard her last spelling word. She knew it by heart, and she quickly answered, "Nest. N-E-S-T. Nest."

"A fine job, Caroline," Miss Morgan complimented her. "You spelled every word correctly."

Caroline smiled shyly back at Miss Morgan. "Thank you, ma'am," she said, feeling every bit as thrilled as she did when Mother or Grandma singled her out for praise.

"You are welcome," Miss Morgan replied. After adding Caroline's point to her team's score, she turned to Elsa. "For your final word, Elsa, please spell 'frog.' "

Tiny lines crept across Elsa's forehead as she closed her eyes and concentrated as hard as she could. " 'F-R-O . . ." she said, then suddenly stopped.

"Yes, Elsa," Miss Morgan encouraged, "F-R-O . . ."

" 'F-R-O . . ." Elsa pushed her bangs out of her eyes and called out triumphantly, *"Gay!"*

The room was silent except for the stout robin that was now strutting along the windowsill whistling a merry tune. Miss Morgan frowned as the silence in the classroom swelled into a burst of laughter from twenty-three young voices. "Enough," Miss Morgan commanded, rapping the bottom of her slate pencil on the table.

Caroline didn't laugh. She didn't smile. She didn't even look at Anna or Martha. Her eyes stayed fixed on Elsa; strange, unfriendly Elsa who was now making up letters for words she didn't know how to spell. Caroline watched as Elsa's blue eyes filled with tears.

"I am sorry, Elsa, that is incorrect," Miss Morgan said over the laughter. The room grew silent again as she swiftly turned away from Elsa and said, "If you can spell the word 'frog,' Caroline, your team will receive an extra point."

As her teammates held their breath, Caroline looked out at the expectant faces on the benches in front of her and halfheartedly spelled, "Frog. F-R-O-G. Frog.'"

"That is correct. Your team receives the point, Caroline."

"*Nein!*" Elsa cried, tears spilling down her cheeks. "Elsa say it! Elsa right!"

As the rest of the classroom waited in stunned silence, Miss Morgan faced her sobbing young student. "Elsa, there is no such letter as 'gay' in the English language, and the only language we speak in this classroom is English. The correct letter is *g*."

"*Nein!* Elsa right!" Elsa sucked in breath and sobs all at once and exclaimed, "Ah-bay-tsay-day-ay-ef-*gay*!" Without another word, she bolted past the packed benches and out the front door of the schoolhouse.

Miss Morgan quickly ended the spelling bee and dismissed the class for dinner. Caroline and Martha walked most of the way home in silence. As they reached the frame house, Caroline realized that she had never even listened to Miss Morgan when she announced the winner of the spelling bee. "Did my team win, Martha?" she asked.

"Fair and square," Martha said, pulling open the door. "You were a real good speller, Caroline."

"Thank you," Caroline answered.

Martha's praise didn't soothe any of the confusion or sadness that Caroline was feeling. For the first time in weeks, she entered the house without marching.

Words

Mother wiped her damp brow and looked up from the pot that was simmering on the black iron stove. "You're just in time for dinner, girls," she said. "Wash up quickly and set the table, please. The boys will be here in no time."

"Yes ma'am," Caroline and Martha answered, heading for the washstand.

"What did your team win today, Caroline?" Mother asked as Caroline and Martha scooped a syrupy dollop of soap from a small tin container that was set beside a bowl of cool water.

"Just a spelling bee," Caroline answered, and began washing her hands. For weeks she had imagined rushing home from school and telling Mother and Grandma how she had stood in front of the whole class and spelled all her words correctly. But she wasn't nearly as happy as she had thought she would be. All she could think about was Elsa's tear-stained face.

"Caroline spelled every word perfectly, Mother," Martha said proudly. "She even spelled one that wasn't supposed to be hers exactly right too! No other speller was near as good."

"Congratulations, Caroline," Mother praised. "Your hard work certainly paid off."

"It sounds like you have good news. Share it with me!" Grandma said as she entered the room, Eliza clinging to one side of her long gray skirt and Thomas tugging on the other.

"Me too," Eliza exclaimed.

"Caroline spelled all her words correctly at school today," Mother explained. "She helped her team win the spelling bee."

"I want to go to school and spell with bees too," Eliza said.

"Soon enough, little one. Right now you must wash up for dinner. You too, Thomas."

Gently squeezing Caroline's shoulder, Grandma whispered, "Good for you, Caroline." Then she took hold of Eliza's and Thomas's hands and guided them toward the washstand.

Within minutes the table was set. Wisps of steam rose from the bowls of bean soup, curling up toward the rafters. Bright-green peas dotted the mounds of yellow summer squash centered on each plate. Every cup was filled with creamy milk, and a fresh crusty loaf of bread waited in the center of the table.

"What's keeping your brothers?" Mother wondered aloud as she lifted Thomas into his chair. "We must eat now or Caroline and Martha will be late getting back to school, so let us give thanks."

Caroline bowed her head and folded her hands as Mother and Grandma prayed aloud. The hot steam rising from the bowl of beans tickled her nose, and all the food on the table smelled delicious. But Caroline did not feel hungry at all.

"Eat up now, Caroline," Mother said before Caroline even noticed that everyone at the table was already eating, "or you'll never get to school in time for the rest of your lessons."

Picking up her fork, Caroline began pushing squash and peas around on her plate. "Yes, ma'am," she answered. She had no appetite for the vegetables, so she dipped her spoon into the beans and lifted it toward her lips, only to turn it over slowly and watch the soup flow back into her bowl.

"You'll not hear a word the schoolteacher says this afternoon if your stomach's complaining, Caroline!" Mother said. "Whatever is the matter? Why aren't you eating?"

"She's still feeling sorry for Elsa, I'll bet," Martha interrupted, her mouth half full of bread. "I didn't feel sorry for her. Not in the least little bit. That girl's never said one nice word to anybody."

"Finish chewing please, Martha. Then tell

me, who is Elsa?" Mother asked curiously.

"She's a girl in school who didn't know how to spell one of her words today. Miss Morgan had Caroline spell the same word instead, and Caroline got every letter right. Elsa was mad as a hornet," Martha said matter-of-factly. "She yelled that her spelling was right, and then she started crying and ran right out of the schoolhouse!"

"Goodness glory!" Mother exclaimed.

"I don't see why anyone should feel sorry for her," Martha continued. "She doesn't talk to anybody even when they're trying to be nice to her, and when she doesn't know how to spell a word, she makes up her very own letters! Least I admit it when I don't know how to spell a word. Seems the right thing to do, after all."

As Martha speared pieces of squash onto her fork, Mother turned her attention to Caroline. "Is all of this true, Caroline?" she asked gently.

"Yes, ma'am," Caroline nodded.

"Why do you feel so sorry for Elsa, then?"

41

"She talks funny, Mother," Caroline answered. "Maybe that's why she doesn't ever want to talk to anybody."

"What do you mean?" Mother asked.

"She says 'gay' instead of *g*," Caroline said. "And she shouts out numbers like 'nine' instead of words! And the only sentence she's ever said was something silly like 'Ah-bay-tsay . . .' "

"Why, she's speaking in German, Caroline." Mother smiled. "She's saying the alphabet, I think!"

"German?"

"German is another language, another way of speaking," Mother explained. "It's every bit as real a language as English. Years ago in Boston, a German family lived upstairs from my dressmaking shop. I often heard their conversation, and it sounded just like what you heard Elsa say today. Listen carefully enough, Caroline, and you'll even hear some folks speaking it in town, especially those just settling in Brookfield. Elsa may not talk to you because she doesn't know how to speak English, girls. That being said," Mother finished, "I expect you'll be extra kind to her. Perhaps you can even help her learn faster."

Martha raised an eyebrow. "How are we s'posed to help her if we don't even know how to talk to her?"

"You may start by being more understanding, Martha," Mother said firmly. "Now both of you, finish eating or you'll never get back to school."

Caroline was hungry now and she took an extra-big bite of beans. The thick soup tasted even better than it looked, and she savored every bite as she thought about Elsa. Maybe Mother was right, and all Elsa needed was someone to teach her how to speak English. Maybe that explained why Elsa was so shy, and why Miss Morgan was so patient with her poor spellings and mispronunciations. Caroline didn't have any idea how to teach somebody English, but as she swallowed her second helping of squash and peas, she was determined to help somehow.

"Well, there you are!" Mother exclaimed as the door to the frame house flew open and

Henry burst in. "You boys should know better than to be late for dinner."

Henry's curls were stuck to his sweaty forehead, and he wiped them out of his eyes as he gasped his news between breaths. "We couldn't help it, Mother. Joseph's hurt."

"Whatever . . ." Mother began as she rushed to the door to help Henry. Leaning heavily on his brother's shoulder, Joseph hopped slowly into the room on one bare foot. His light-brown hair was caked with dirt, and his gray cotton shirt was stained. Looking closely at her oldest brother's face, Caroline could tell he was holding back tears.

"Sit here, Joseph." Grandma quickly stood up as Mother and Henry helped him hobble to the table.

"It hurts considerable, but it's not broken, I don't think." Joseph gritted his teeth and spoke as if every word pained him.

Once he was safely in the chair and balancing his foot above the wooden floorboards, Mother knelt down and gently pressed her fingertips around Joseph's foot and ankle. "How in the world . . . ?" she began.

"I was out working by the corn," Henry interrupted. "One minute Joseph's a couple rows ahead of me, pulling weeds. Next minute he's facedown on top of a whole pile of beans, crying out something awful! Took near forever to get him up off the dirt and over to the house."

"There was a hole dug deep in the ground." Joseph frowned. "I never saw it there before."

"We filled it in right off the reel," Henry said. "Not a body will turn their ankle there again."

"You'll not be walking on this ankle anytime soon, I'm afraid." Mother looked up at Joseph, her voice full of concern. "It's already swollen, and I fear it'll get worse yet. Martha, as soon as you finish eating, I want you to run to the Carpenters' and see if Mr. Carpenter can come take a look. If you have trouble finding him, go to town and find Dr. Hatch. We must be certain that Joseph hasn't broken a bone."

"Yes, ma'am!" Martha answered, digging into her soup.

"I will sit with Joseph until Mr. Carpenter arrives," Mother continued. "Henry, you can finish your brother's chores. I'm sorry, Caroline, but you'll have to return to the schoolhouse by yourself this afternoon."

"I could stay home too, Mother, and help with Joseph's chores," Caroline offered. She had never gone to school by herself and was certain that she wouldn't be able to pay attention to her lessons when she was so concerned about her brother.

"No, Caroline," Mother said. "Finish your dinner and hurry back to the schoolhouse. No sense in both you and Martha missing your afternoon lessons. Tell Miss Morgan why Martha is staying at home."

Martha grinned at Caroline and Caroline scrunched up her nose in response as they both finished dinner. Once the dish dresser was again full of clean, dry dishes, Caroline tied on her bonnet and started for the door.

"If I were you, I'd take the shortcut through the back meadow instead of going through town," Henry suggested. "No chance you'll be late then."

"But the marsh," Caroline said, then hesitated. "I don't want to get my dress all wet and dirty before I go back to school."

"It's mostly dried up," Henry answered. "You'll be able to jump across any wet spots, easy."

Caroline said good-bye to her brother, stepped out into the hot July afternoon, and set off for school. The earth was hot and dusty. Hard, crusty dirt pebbles and stones jabbed her bare feet as she hurried past the woodpile, past the garden, past the barn, and off through the meadows and marshland that bordered the Quiners' land. Henry was right after all, Caroline thought as she wove between tall, stringy blades of dry grass and fuzzy brown cattails. Usually there were shallow pools of water or damp, sticky mud all around, but today the soil was dry in the marshes too. Even the wide cracks in the dirt, darting off in all directions beneath Caroline's toes, were dried inside and out.

As she neared the narrow creek that ran alongside their land, Caroline breathed a sigh of relief. The tiny creek supplied much of their water, and it was still rolling along, gurgling and sparkling in the sunlight, though Caroline noticed it moved much less busily than usual.

When she finally reached the creek's narrowest point, Caroline lifted the hem of her dress and climbed onto the three-boulder path that cut across the brook. Spreading her arms as far apart as possible, Caroline steadied herself on a smooth, flat rock and dipped her toes into the cool, bubbling water. A miniature rainbow mist hovered above the water droplets splashing off the sides of the boulders. Caroline bent down slowly and tried to touch the rainbow, but she couldn't reach it. At that very moment she heard someone singing.

It was a girl's voice, humming above the gurgling water. Caroline straightened up slowly and searched the creek bed for the sound. There, seated beneath a cluster of cattails, was Elsa, busily twisting stems into long yellow braids.

Elsa saw Caroline at the very same moment. Her happy, peaceful face filled with fear, and she quickly gathered up her pile of cattail braids, scrambled to her feet, and turned to flee.

"Wait!" Caroline hollered. "Please, Elsa! Wait!"

Elsa began to run, but Caroline scurried over the boulders and dashed after her. Within moments she caught Elsa by the sleeve.

"Please, wait!" Caroline begged, trying to catch her breath.

Elsa shook her arm away from Caroline and stood looking at her defiantly.

"I know you were right at the spelling bee today," Caroline began. "My mother told me you were speaking German. I didn't know you couldn't speak English."

Pushing her thick bangs out of her eyes, Elsa stared at Caroline, her gaze unwavering. "Elsa right," she finally said.

"Yes, I know." Caroline smiled. "I'm sorry, Elsa. About the spelling bee, I mean."

Elsa didn't speak and Caroline quickly filled in the silence. "May I walk back to the schoolhouse with you? Martha had to stay home, so I'm all alone and . . ." Pausing, Caroline realized that Elsa didn't know what she was saying, so she stopped talking.

"Elsa. No. Go," Elsa said slowly.

"But you must go back!" Caroline exclaimed. "You can sit next to me and Anna, and we'll try to help you learn words as best we can! Please, Elsa. We must go now or we'll be late getting back!"

Caroline reached out toward Elsa. Elsa stared at her for many moments before she switched her cattail braids from one hand to the other and took Caroline's hand. Together they hurried out of the marsh, across another wide meadow, up a steep hill, and on toward the schoolhouse, chattering the whole way.

"Sun," Caroline said, squinting up at the sky.

"*Sonne,*" Elsa answered. "Sun."

"Tree," Caroline said, pointing at a maple in their path.

"*Baum,*" Elsa answered. "Terr-ee."

"Grass," Caroline said, kneeling down and running her hands over a thick patch of dry grass.

"*Gras,*" Elsa repeated. "Gr-a-ss."

"Right!" Caroline exclaimed proudly and pulled a black-eyed Susan out of the ground to show Elsa. "Flower," she said slowly, waiting for Elsa's response.

"*Blume!*" Elsa laughed back. "F . . . flow-err!"

By the time Caroline and Elsa ran up the schoolhouse steps, Elsa had learned a dozen new words. Caroline had discovered a new friend.

Wolf

For almost a week, Joseph hobbled around on his sprained ankle, telling his younger brother and sisters how to do his chores. Caroline and Martha pulled weeds from the garden, fetched fresh water from the creek, and carried apronful after apronful of wood chips and sticks to the wood box. Henry spent the days splitting logs and carting them into the house. Every evening when he dropped into his chair for supper, he rubbed his sore hands together and complained, "Been close to a coon's age since you hurt that ankle,

Joseph. Isn't it any better yet?"

"Henry Odin Quiner!" Mother said sternly. "Your brother will be back to work when his ankle is fully healed. Not a day sooner."

One evening, though, Joseph answered Henry's question before Mother had a chance to respond. "Feels mostly fine, Henry," he said. "I'll split the firewood tomorrow if you'll haul the water from the creek. Don't need to do much walking if I'm splitting logs."

"Are you certain, Joseph?" Mother asked. "Dr. Hatch says not to walk on it too soon. You'll only make it worse."

"No lick about it, Mother," Joseph answered determinedly. "I can work in the garden too. I'll just sit or kneel when I'm thinning the vegetables."

Dimples flashing for the first time in days, Henry cried out, "Hallelujah!" and stuffed a huge chunk of corn bread into his mouth.

"Fine, then, Joseph," Mother agreed. "You're the best judge. Caroline and Martha don't have school tomorrow, so they can help you and Henry."

Joseph was as good as his word. The next morning when Caroline passed the woodpile on her way to feed the chickens, Joseph's metal ax was flashing as he drove it into one heavy log after another. Caroline waved and ran off toward the barn, thinking that it would take her brother most of the day just to chop the towering pile of logs down to his size.

"Where've you been, little Brownbraid?" Henry was crouched in the center room of the barn, pouring water from a wooden bucket into a trough for the Quiners' big pig, Hog. The knees of his trousers were soiled, and his bare feet were caked with dirt and straw. "Those chickens have 'bout squawked their little red heads off, waiting for you to let them loose and feed them."

"They're always fussing this time of morning," Caroline answered. Picking up an empty bucket, she hurried across the straw-covered dirt floor to the grain bin.

"I'll get it for you," Henry said cheerfully, opening the lid. "If you hurry up and finish with the chickens, you can come along with me. I could use your help."

Caroline scooped up two dusty handfuls of grain and poured them into the bucket. "Help with what?" she asked curiously.

"I need an extra hand down by the creek."

Caroline's heart sank. Mother had said she and Martha had to help their brothers, but hauling water from the creek was Caroline's least favorite chore, and she'd been helping with it every day since Joseph hurt his ankle. Her arms ached, her back hurt, and a line of tiny blisters cut across the insides of her fingers where she had carried the handle of bucket after bucket. She couldn't bear the thought of one more trip to the creek. "Oh, Henry," Caroline pleaded, "couldn't I please help with something else?"

"You won't have to carry a single bucket of water," Henry assured her. "Your only job will be to fill all the baskets you can carry with every wild, juicy berry that I don't eat first!"

"Really, Henry?" Caroline cried.

"You should see them today, Caroline! The banks of the creek are loaded with berries. I went to fetch water for Hog first thing this morning, and I ate as many as I could get my hands on, and there are plenty more to spare! I say we collect a couple of baskets before dinner and surprise Mother."

"Oh, yes, I'll help with that!" Caroline agreed happily.

"Well, hurry up and we're off!"

Caroline clapped gleefully and began tossing handfuls of grain from the bin into the bucket. She flew through her chores in no time and met Henry at the woodpile, two empty baskets swinging on each arm.

"We'll be back before dinner," Henry called out to Joseph as he leaned his ax against the woodpile and reached for two of the baskets. "Let's get a move on, little Brownbraid," he added with a wink. "I've been thinking about those berries all morning!"

The meadow behind the Quiners' barn was greener and softer than it had been the afternoon when Caroline had last traveled through it and found Elsa stringing cattail braids. Thunderstorms had rolled through Brookfield half a dozen times since then, and the pelting rain had quenched the cracked, thirsty soil and turned the grass fresh and lush again.

Breathing in the sweet smell of the meadow, Caroline struggled to keep up with Henry's long strides. Lacy long-stemmed flowers, grandly displaying clusters of tiny white blossoms, brushed her skirt at every step. Caroline was fascinated by the delicate design of the Queen Anne's lace and longed to stop and pick a small bouquet. But there wasn't time. She and Henry had work to do.

Soon the meadow thinned and dampened into marsh. Henry and Caroline headed east, trudging along the soft, soggy earth until they were well past the three-boulder bridge that cut across the creek.

"We can start picking any time now," Henry said, "though there are more and more berries the farther along we go."

Twirling around, Caroline wasn't certain where to begin. Wild raspberry and elderberry bushes grew all along the edge of the meadow, their tangled branches heavy with ripe, dark berries. Chokecherries swung from small trees and littered the ground. Closer to the earth, blueberry bushes brimmed with clusters of ripening berries. Caroline could not imagine how there could possibly be more berries farther along. Already there were more berries right in front of her than she had ever seen.

"Which ones should we pick?" Caroline asked.

"Most anything you see," Henry answered, and began pulling clusters of blueberries from their bushes. "Mother will use every berry we bring her, I bet. I'll fill my baskets with blueberries and elderberries. You pick the raspberries and chokecherries." Henry's mouth was now full of blueberries, and Caroline could hardly understand him as he added, "Don't pick any blackberries yet. They're still too green and they'll pucker up your mouth."

"I won't," Caroline assured him.

"We don't have much time before we have to head back for dinner," Henry continued, "so I say we race. First one to fill their baskets wins!"

In a flash, Henry was off to another blueberry patch. Caroline turned to the first wild raspberry bush she saw, and swiftly picked berry after berry, determined to beat Henry. The sweet pink juice stained her fingers as she tugged the berries from the bush and dropped them gently in her basket, and the rich, syrupy smell of the fruit was intoxicating. Caroline tried as hard as she could to think of picking berries instead of eating them. But once half her basket was filled with the wild raspberries, she couldn't resist any longer. Race or no race, the next three picks ended up in her mouth.

As Caroline closed her eyes and savored the sweet fruit, something rustled in the bushes behind her. She looked around for Henry, hoping he hadn't already finished filling his baskets. But Henry was not there.

Caroline straightened up slowly. The tall grass stood still and the humid air hung heavy and silent. Caroline didn't see anyone, but she was certain that she had heard the rustling noises. "Henry?" she called out sternly, thinking her brother was playing a joke on her. Henry would do almost anything to win a race. "Henry Odin Quiner, you come out now so I can see you!"

Suddenly the rustling began again behind her and Caroline whirled around, expecting Henry to jump up and shout, "Scared you!" Instead, she found a furry gray-and-black face, a pointed muzzle, and two dark-brown eyes looking up at her from a few feet away. Her throat tightened and her heart began to pound. Caroline knew it was a wolf.

"Don't move."

Caroline heard Henry's voice clearly, but he was too far back to step in before the wolf attacked. Biting her lip to keep it from shaking, she stared at the wolf's long face. His body was lean and muscular, and his fur was almost as dark as his eyes. He quietly panted, waving his bushy tail and watching her.

"Easy, boy."

Henry's voice was closer now, and Caroline

slowly lowered her basket to the ground. Standing perfectly still, she waited what seemed like hours as Henry inched his way through the grass.

The wolf had his own plans. Without taking his eyes off Caroline, he began moving toward her, his body crouched low to the ground. Caroline decided to run, but her bare feet would not move. She was trembling all over and frozen in place. Clenching her fists, she closed her eyes so tightly, it hurt.

"Easy, boy." Henry's voice was right behind her now, but Caroline still couldn't move. It wasn't until she felt a sticky tongue on her fingers that she finally opened her eyes. Standing right beside her, his tail wagging, the wolf was licking her fingers.

"I reckon you didn't need me after all," Henry said as he knelt down on the ground beside Caroline. "Good boy. That's a good old boy," he told the wolf. Gently Henry reached out and rubbed the back of his hand up and down the animal's long gray nose. "Where did you come from, huh? Who do you belong to?" he asked.

"You don't think somebody owns him, Henry!" Caroline said with great relief and wonder. As long as she could remember, wolves had howled mournfully outside her house while she was trying to fall asleep. She'd heard stories about wolves that suddenly appeared in folks' kitchens or killed all their chickens, and even Father had once been attacked by a wolf. But Caroline had never heard any talk or story about a friendly wolf.

"I imagine he belonged to somebody at one time or another. He isn't afraid of you. Or me either, for that matter," Henry mused.

"I never heard of anybody owning a wolf before," Caroline said. "Not even a nice one like him."

Tossing his head back, Henry laughed up at the sky so delightedly that his whole body shook. "So that's why you were so frightened," he cried out, gulping for air. "Silly Caroline! This isn't a wolf! He's a dog, is all, and most likely came to town with some folks who up and left without taking him along to the next place."

Caroline didn't know whether to giggle or cry. She was so relieved, she didn't even care that Henry was laughing at her. "He looks just like a wolf, Henry!" she said defensively.

"He does," Henry admitted, "and if he follows us home and Mother lets us keep him, I think we ought to call him Wolf."

"We haven't had a dog since Father left," Caroline said. Their dog, Bones, had disappeared almost two years ago on the same day Father had set sail on a schooner. The schooner had capsized in a terrible storm, and Father had never returned home. Bones didn't come back either, and Mother concluded that Bones must have followed Father onto the ship.

Henry's voice grew softer, and he patted the dog's thick brown coat. "Maybe you can be our new dog, Wolf, if you don't already have a family of your own. My sister and me will be heading home soon as we fill our baskets. You're welcome to come along if you like." Turning to Caroline, Henry added, "Fill your baskets as high as you can, little Brownbraid, so Mother will be extra pleased."

Caroline filled her baskets so high that a plump, juicy berry or two tumbled out of each basket with almost every step she took on the way home. Wolf remained close by, walking along and gobbling up every stray berry that fell to the ground. As Caroline and Henry neared the little frame house, Wolf was still at Caroline's side.

"He's followed us all the way home. I bet he doesn't have any other place to go," Henry said happily. "We'll keep him in the barn until Mother says he can stay. You go on ahead, Caroline. And don't tell Mother about the dog till I get there!"

Setting her baskets on the ground, Caroline knelt down in front of Wolf. "I hope you'll be able to stay!" she whispered and hugged him so tight, she could feel his cold, wet nose against her cheek. Wolf's soft brown eyes followed her every move, and he scrambled after her as she lifted her baskets and headed to the house.

"Whoa!" Henry cried, grabbing him tightly. "You can't come to dinner just yet."

"Hurry up, Henry!" Caroline urged as she neared the little frame house. "I can't wait to tell Mother!"

Mother greeted Caroline with a quick "Where have you and Henry-O been?" Before Caroline could answer, Mother exclaimed, "Goodness glory! Have you ever seen so many fine berries?"

Caroline was happy to see Mother's smile spread across her face. But she wasn't thinking about the berries right now. There was a much bigger surprise waiting in the barn.

Critters

Henry ran into the house just as Grandma was pouring milk into the tin cups and Martha was lifting Thomas onto his chair.

"More berries!" Mother cried when Henry handed her his baskets. "Why, we'll have to spend the next two days preserving them!"

"If it's all the same to you, Charlotte," Grandma said, "I'll wash some of those berries right now. They'll make a lovely dessert."

"That would be fine, Mother Quiner," Mother agreed.

"Eat!" Thomas bounced in his chair, waving his spoon up and down. "Eat, now."

Mother patted his head and gently shushed him. "As soon as Grandma finishes, Thomas."

"No, no," Grandma insisted, "you all go ahead and begin. This won't take but a minute or two."

"Then we're only missing Joseph," Mother said. "He told me he'd be delayed awhile, so I'll keep his dinner hot, and the rest of us can eat." Tipping a ladleful of steamy succotash into Thomas's bowl, Mother asked, "Were you able to finish your chores, children? Or did berry picking take up your whole morning?"

"No, ma'am," Caroline replied quickly. "We finished all our work before we went to the creek."

"Good." Without looking up from the corn-and-bean mixture she was pouring, Mother continued, "What's got your tongue, Henry-O?"

Startled, Henry sat up straight. "Pardon me, ma'am?"

"You haven't said a word since you came through that door," Mother noted. "You washed up without any reminder, and you even combed your hair out of your face. Is something wrong?"

"I'm just thinking, is all," he responded very politely, glancing sideways at Caroline.

"Thinking about what?" Mother inquired.

"Well, it seems to me that we should get us a new dog."

"And why is that?" Mother sounded surprised, but she kept right on spooning out the succotash. Caroline suddenly felt very warm. Shifting in her seat, she dabbed her napkin at the back of her neck, which was sticky beneath her collar.

"We haven't had one around here since old Bones up and left 'most two years ago. It would be useful to have another, I think," Henry continued thoughtfully.

"What's made you consider such a thing?" Mother asked. Caroline watched her face closely, looking for any sign that Mother agreed or disagreed with Henry. But she didn't see any.

"Nothing special, ma'am," Henry fibbed, avoiding Caroline's glance. "But let's just say if we found a dog, a real nice dog, and he didn't belong to anybody partic'lar . . . It would be all right if he were to stay here with us and be our new dog, wouldn't it?"

"You know full well that we didn't get another dog after Bones disappeared because we couldn't feed one, Henry. It's hard enough keeping food on the table for all the children in this family. No sense in taking on another mouth to feed." Mother's tone now clearly told Caroline that the discussion was over. With a sigh of disappointment, Caroline looked over at her brother.

"What if the dog didn't eat much?" Henry persisted. "What if I made sure he only ate leftover table scraps or berries or other such things I could find for him?"

"We don't have leftover table scraps, Henry-O," Mother said. "And it makes no sense to keep an animal that we cannot keep fed and healthy. It isn't fair to the poor dog. Now where is it, Henry-O? Have you found a dog?"

"Yes, ma'am," Henry admitted guiltily.

"Where did you find him?"

"Down by the creek. Caroline thought he was a wolf," Henry explained. "Scared her but good."

"So you've seen this dog also, Caroline?" Mother asked.

"Yes, Mother," Caroline murmured.

"I want to see him!" Eliza said eagerly.

"I always miss everything!" Martha grumbled.

"How do you know he doesn't already have a family?" Mother asked.

"He found Caroline picking her berries, and he never left her side till I shut him in the barn. He didn't seem to have anywhere to go the whole time we were down by the creek, and he followed us all the way home, never once looking back. He's real pretty, Mother. He's gray and black, and very strong and—"

"I've heard enough," Mother interrupted firmly. "As soon as you finish your dinner, I want you to set that dog free. He'll find another family that can feed him and care for him better than we can."

"Yes, ma'am," Henry answered, staring intently at his plate so no one at the table could see his disappointment.

Caroline looked down at her bowl of corn and beans while Mother gave thanks. "May I please go with Henry when he sends Wolf away?" she asked when Mother finished.

"Yes you may, Caroline," Mother answered kindly. "Take heart, children. This won't be the last stray you'll find. Sooner or later we'll be able to take on another animal. I also would like another dog. Old Bones was a fine companion."

"Mother?" Joseph had stepped into the room and was standing by the door. His face was sweaty and smudged with dirt, and he looked worried.

"Yes, Joseph," Mother's back remained turned to him while she wiped some succotash off Thomas's cheek.

"I need you in the garden as soon as you're able to come." Joseph's voice was so serious that Caroline knew something awful had happened.

72

"What is it?" Mother spun around on her chair.

"Holes. Holes just like the one I turned my ankle on, but they're all over the ground now. And the vegetables"—Joseph stumbled over his words—"a lot of the leaves have turned yellow and dry. The vegetables are dying," he said, his voice cracking, "but I can't figure why. They've had plenty of sun and water."

"Lord help us," Mother said softly. "Woodchucks. I should have known. I should have known the day you fell."

"It can't be woodchucks," Joseph countered. "How'd they ever get through the fence? I can't find a single break in it."

Setting her fork on the table, Mother stood up at once. "Finish your meal, children. Henry, as soon as you're done, I want you out in the garden."

"I could help too, Mother," Martha said hopefully.

"No, you stay and help Grandma, please."

"I always have to stay and help!" Martha complained.

"And you do now, as well." Mother's stern voice worried Caroline. "Be good girls and help clean up the dishes as quickly as possible. We'll come for you if we need your help." With a quick pat on Thomas's head, she and Joseph left the house.

Henry gulped down the rest of his meal and jumped up from his chair. "I'm going, now, Grandma," he announced, and scrambled out the door.

Caroline and Martha washed and dried the dishes in silence. Martha grumbled about staying inside, and Caroline prayed that all the vegetables were still alive. Just last fall, a terrible frost had stripped all the life from their vegetable garden, and she couldn't bear the thought of seeing it happen again.

The dishes were dry and Caroline was pushing the chairs back where they belonged when Henry stuck his head through the open door. "Mother says to come help if you're finished with the dishes," he told Caroline and Martha.

"Let's go!" Martha cried, and ran out of the house with Caroline close behind.

A heavy, humid breeze, blowing from the north like sticky, hot breath, hit Caroline full in the face as she ran toward the garden. Mother, Joseph, and Henry were kneeling in different rows, filling in the garden's gaping holes with dirt.

"We're here!" Martha announced as she and Caroline stepped over the short stick fence.

Mother rubbed the back of her hand over her forehead. "Find every hole you can, fill it with dirt, and pat it down hard," she explained. "The critters have dug mighty deep holes, so be careful not to step into one and turn your ankle. Martha, start with a row of corn. Caroline, begin down by the squash."

"Are the vegetables all lost again, Mother?" Caroline asked.

"I don't know just yet," Mother said grimly. "These woodchucks dig their burrows and start eating the vegetables from the bottom up. There's no telling how many we'll lose, since it's nearly impossible to see the roots or figure out how widespread the burrows are. The most important thing now is to fill up their holes, and secure the fence so that they can't get in again. Hurry along now, Caroline. We must work as quickly as possible."

Nodding, Caroline turned and walked cautiously alongside the stick fence to the back of the garden, searching the ground for holes. Corn stalks swayed back and forth in the breeze, and Caroline looked them over quickly as she passed. Except for a few tips of leaves that had turned brown, the corn looked as green and alive as ever.

Kneeling down beside the first hole she found, Caroline noticed that the squash hadn't been so lucky. Vines sprawled freely, as if they intended to take over the whole garden, but their broad, furry leaves had begun to droop and turn a dingy olive green.

Caroline lifted a sagging leaf, her cheeks flushing with anger. "Shame on you, woodchucks, crawling into our garden and eating vegetables that don't belong to you," she exclaimed. "Why can't you just run down to the creek and eat all those berries that are there for the taking? Well, I'll show you!"

With that, she pushed dirt into the hole until it was filled and the ground was level once again.

Caroline filled the other three holes that she found among the rows of squash. As soon as each burrow was filled in, she firmly pressed and patted the soil covering it, then pounded it down with her fists. Finally, she stood up and stomped her bare feet over the top until she was certain that no critter underneath could escape. "There!" she huffed, with one final stomp.

Brushing the dirt off her apron, Caroline hurried back toward the front of the garden. Mother was busy working in a row of pumpkins. Deep grooves and scratches marred the pumpkins' hard green skin, and Caroline knew without asking that the woodchucks had been gnawing at them. Joseph was crouched down close by, examining the bottom of the stick fence. "Did you find the place where the critters got in, Joseph?" Caroline asked hopefully.

"This is it," Joseph muttered with disgust. "The varmints dug a burrow right through the bottom of the fence without breaking a single stick. It's no wonder I couldn't find any hole in the fence."

"Whoop! I got one!" Henry shrieked from the back corner of the garden. "There! It's heading for those trees!"

Caroline took Joseph's arm and helped him hop down a row of beans that had been nibbled from one end to the other. Henry had hurtled the fence and was racing after a small brown creature that was scuttling toward the three maple trees that towered over one side of the barn.

"Run, Henry!" Joseph hollered.

"What's all the commotion?" Mother was frowning as she raised her skirt above her ankles and stepped over row after row of plants to join Caroline and Joseph.

Martha was only a step behind. "Where's Henry going?" she asked.

"He spotted a woodchuck running out of the garden, and he's gone after it," Caroline explained excitedly.

"Dash it all!" Joseph cried in disbelief as he watched Henry rushing from tree to tree, searching the tall leafy branches for the woodchuck. "I don't think he knows which tree the critter's got into. I have to go help him find it."

"Not on that ankle you don't," Mother said.

"Wait!" Martha exclaimed as Henry turned and ran into the barn. "Where's he going now?"

"How do I know?" Joseph cried out angrily. "It's getting away!"

"Henry's going into the barn," Caroline said, her heart pounding so fast, she could barely hear her own words. "He's getting Wolf!"

The moment she finished speaking, Henry ran out of the barn carrying a long stick. Wolf was beside him. When they reached the three maples, Wolf circled the trunk of each tree and then began leaping about the bottom of the center tree, barking sharply.

Reaching his stick high up into the leafy branches, Henry began poking around vigorously. The woodchuck fell from the tree with a thud. Wolf charged at it and snapped his jaws around the rodent's thick, furry neck. Caroline caught her breath as the woodchuck fell limp and Henry shouted, "We sure fixed his flint, Wolf! Atta boy!"

"Who's Wolf?" Joseph asked, confused. "Where'd he come from?"

"I don't know where he came from Joseph," Mother admitted, shaking her head, "but I think he may become our new dog."

"Oh please, Mother!" Caroline cried. "May we keep him then?"

"Go and tell your brother that the dog stays in the barn, Caroline, and it's his job to make sure he gets enough food," Mother ordered. With a smile she added, "And no table scraps!"

Joyfully, Caroline stepped over the fence and ran off to the side of the barn to hug Wolf and tell Henry the wonderful news.

"Guess those woodchucks are good for something, after all." Henry grinned.

Caroline had to agree.

Old Dan Tucker

Soon autumn wrung the rich green shade from the maple leaves and colored them in with crimson and gold. Every afternoon Caroline and Martha, Henry and Joseph, filled bucket after bucket with cucumbers, peas, lima beans, corn, sweet potatoes, squash, onions, turnips, and potatoes. The woodchucks had scurried off to dig new burrows far away from Wolf, and the Quiners had firmly packed all their old tunnels with dirt. In the end, only one small section of turnips and sweet potatoes, and a full row of beans, had been lost to the gnawing woodchucks. Before every meal, Mother gave thanks for their good fortune and prayed that the first frost would hold off until all their vegetables were fully ripened and harvested.

One evening as Caroline finished drying the last drops of water off a tin cup, Mother announced, "We'll spend the rest of the week pickling and preserving the fresh vegetables for winter." Turning to Joseph and Henry, who were whittling away small bits of kindling in front of the wood box, she added, "The girls and I will take Thomas along tomorrow when we go to the general store. You can get your chores done, boys, without the baby getting underfoot."

"I'm a baby!" Thomas repeated very seriously.

"I'm happy to join you, Charlotte," Grandma spoke up quickly. She was seated beside the sewing table, her fingers shaking slightly as she pulled her needle and thread through the black woolen trousers she was mending. "You'll all just have to walk a bit slower if I come along," she added with a gentle smile.

"I had hoped you would stay and rest some, Mother Quiner," Mother suggested. "You've been caring for the little ones and cooking dinner most days while the rest of us have tended to the harvest. You're looking far too tired," she added in a low tone that Caroline overheard.

"You mustn't worry so, Charlotte," Grandma answered quickly.

"And you must rest," Mother said. "It's no trouble to bring Eliza and Thomas along. Caroline and Martha will watch out for them."

"I'll stay behind and get dinner then," Grandma decided. "A fresh vegetable stew should do just fine. I'll have it ready when you return."

"As you wish," Mother relented with a sigh. "Joseph, you bring in the vegetables Grandma needs tomorrow morning," she instructed. "I don't want her carrying any heavy bushels."

"Yes, ma'am," Joseph promised.

The following morning as Mother, Caroline, and Martha bustled about, tying bonnet strings and straightening ribbons, Joseph set a basket overflowing with colorful vegetables on the table. "Here you are, Grandma," he said cheerfully, disappearing with a quick good-bye.

Mother looked over the children one by one, until she was satisfied that they were neat and clean. Then she picked up a clay crock that was lightly covered with greased brown paper and tied with a string, explaining, "We must stop at the Carpenters' on our way to the general store. Mrs. Carpenter's come down with fever. I'm hoping this soup will help her some."

"May I carry it, Mother?" Caroline reached for the crock eagerly.

"Oh no, please, Mother!" Martha jumped in. "I want to carry the soup!"

"Caroline asked first, Martha," Mother said. "You may help me carry along the shirts I've mended for Mr. Porter. Then we'll each have a free hand for Thomas and Eliza."

Caroline watched as Martha's brow crinkled angrily. "I don't want to carry shirts," she muttered through clenched teeth. "I want to carry the soup!"

Clutching the bottom of the clay crock even tighter, Caroline hugged it close against her apron. She wasn't about to give up the soup, no matter how much Martha wanted it. After all, she had asked to carry it first.

"Fine, Martha," Mother answered patiently. "I'll carry the shirts, and you may hold on to both Eliza *and* Thomas. Come along now, all of you." Mother's tone made it clear that she was not about to change her mind. Glaring at Caroline, Martha slipped her fingers around Eliza's and Thomas's and followed Mother out of the frame house in a huff. Holding back a giggle, Caroline smiled to herself as the family headed down the dirt road toward town.

The sun rose slowly through rolling clouds that were tinted a soft gray. The roadsides and meadows were awash in amber and lavender as goldenrod and asters bid the summer farewell. Cool and crisp, the late-September breeze lifted crimson and orange leaves off their branches and sent them pirouetting slowly down to earth.

Walking along behind her family for the half mile to the Carpenters', Caroline held the crock tightly, balancing it carefully so it wouldn't spill. She tried to concentrate on the soup and not let the lovely fall day dampen her spirits, but she couldn't help feeling a little bit sad. Father had loved autumn more than any other season, and Caroline always missed him most at this time of year.

Flocks of birds sailed high above, their black wings shifting gracefully as they crisscrossed the sky. Happily distracted, Caroline watched the squawking birds flip, dip, and swirl until the family arrived at the Carpenters' frame house.

"Good morning, Benjamin," Mother called out cheerfully.

Mr. Carpenter was bending down in front of his wagon, busily hammering a spoke of one wagon wheel. "Sakes alive!" he exclaimed, a grin brightening his face. "If it isn't you, Charlotte!" He slapped his knees and walked with long strides to the dirt road, pushing his sleeves up to his elbows. "Charlotte

86

and all the Quiner ladies looking peart as always! What brings you here so early this morn?"

"We came to see about Sarah," Mother said. "Has the fever broken yet?"

"She's more comfortable than yesterday, I suspect," Mr. Carpenter replied, his voice growing serious. "I can't be sure though, Charlotte. She's still too weak to eat or drink, and she says her head aches something awful. The good doctor Hatch left not twenty minutes ago. Told me to get her some medicine. I'm off to town soon as I fix this wheel."

"I'd be happy to bring it back for you," Mother offered. "We're on our way to the general store right now. We stopped to bring this soup for Sarah."

Caroline stepped forward and handed Mr. Carpenter the clay crock. "I carried it all the way from our house." She smiled up at him. "There's enough soup for you and Charlie, too."

"If half of it didn't spill already," Martha said under her breath.

"I didn't spill one drop!" Caroline shot back. "You're just mad because *I* got to carry the soup instead of *you*!"

"Girls!" Mother exclaimed.

"This must be very extraordinary soup to cause such a fuss," Mr. Carpenter interrupted. "Thank you kindly, little Brownbraid, for bringing it all this way."

"You're welcome, sir." Caroline adjusted her bonnet and glanced sideways at Martha with a satisfied smile.

"Shall I take a moment to see Sarah before we leave?" Mother asked.

Mr. Carpenter shook his head gravely. "Hatch says she's not contagious, but we should keep her quiet and resting until the fever's broke. Charlie will stay with Sarah while I go to town. If you don't mind the company, I'll leave this wagon wheel until later and walk along with you."

"Surely we could save you some trouble and bring the medicine back, Benjamin," Mother urged again.

"I could use a walk and some good company,

Charlotte," Mr. Carpenter insisted. "Wait just a minute while I bring the soup inside and tell Charlie I'm going."

"I wish we all could go along and say hello," Martha said wistfully as Mr. Carpenter disappeared into his house.

"You heard Mr. Carpenter. Best that we let Mrs. Carpenter rest," Mother cautioned. "The ague's nothing to fiddle with."

Caroline had never before seen Mr. Carpenter's face so lined with worry, and she suddenly felt sorry for carrying on with Martha. "Will Mrs. Carpenter get better?" she asked Mother.

"If the Lord so desires," Mother answered.

Once they were on their way again, everyone's mood brightened. Carrying Thomas on his broad shoulders, Mr. Carpenter told scary stories and puzzled the girls with silly riddles and jokes. When they finally arrived at the crossroads of town, he and Mother led the children across deep ruts in the dirt road, weaving in and out of the small circles of chattering townsfolk. Mr. Carpenter waved and called out a loud hello to the wagonmaker and the black-smith before he stopped in front of the general store and swung Thomas down from his shoulders. "I'll stay with the children till you finish getting your goods, Charlotte," he said. "Please tell Porter I'm coming in for Sarah's medicine, so he'll have the tonic ready soon as I go in. Hatch called the medicine 'Dr. Osgood's chologogue,' or something of the sort."

"Of course," Mother said. "I'll take Thomas along, since he's bound to be the most trouble. The rest of you stay with Mr. Carpenter and be quiet little ladies, please."

"Yes, ma'am," Caroline, Martha, and Eliza answered.

Mr. Carpenter turned to the girls as Mother entered the general store. "All right with you if we go watch Carleton and Lake battle at the checkerboard?" he asked with a wink.

"Oh, yes!" Caroline clapped.

"Oh, please, Mr. Ben!" Martha echoed.

"Come along then." Mr. Carpenter chuckled and crossed to the far corner of the stoop, where two men sat hunched over a knotty pine table, surrounded by a small cluster of their neighbors. The top of the table had been carved into a checkerboard. Thick checkers whittled out of dark wood were scattered about the board and stacked on the far corners of the table. Half of the checkers had been dyed a rusty red.

Caroline stood on her tiptoes and studied the two men playing checkers. The older man, Mr. Lake, had a scruffy black beard that was flecked with gray, and bushy sideburns that curled up into his shiny, slicked-back hair. The sides of his large black coat hung to the floor, and Caroline could barely see the wooden stool straining beneath him to support his weight. Across the table, Mr. Carleton watched his opponent anxiously. He had a tightly clipped beard and a lock of finely brushed hair that curved into a cowlick above his forehead. Each time Mr. Lake lifted a black checker between his plump fingers and skipped one of Mr. Carleton's red checkers, Mr. Carleton wrinkled his pointy nose and exclaimed, "Pshaw! Darn you, Lake!" Caroline soon decided that watching these two men play checkers was just the same as watching a match between Henry and Joseph, except her brothers' checkers were only made of corncobs.

Greeting the two men with gentle slaps on the shoulders, Mr. Carpenter kindly chided, "Got yourselves an audience, gents! Now sit back and show these young ladies how to play checkers without all that complaining, or I'll be obliged to show them myself!"

Concentrating intently, the two contestants shifted on their chairs without glancing up at Mr. Carpenter or the girls. Caroline, Martha, and Eliza edged their way in beside the table. Though she kept quiet, Caroline soon found herself rooting for Mr. Carleton. He was, after all, playing with the red checkers, and losing them far too quickly to Mr. Lake.

"Won't be long, little Brownbraid, 'fore Carleton's licked by Lake and leaves us, ladies and gents, the loser," Mr. Carpenter quipped as he knelt behind the girls. "Let's get on back to the door, now. No telling when your mother might walk out, and I imagine she won't be happy seeing her young ladies cheering on a bunch of quibbling men."

Caroline glanced toward the door of the general store and then back up at Mr. Carpenter. "Oh please, Mr. Ben," she begged, "couldn't we please stay one more minute, just to see who wins?"

"We should listen to Mr. Ben, Caroline," Martha said sweetly. "Come along, Eliza."

Caroline watched in disbelief as Martha took her little sister's hand and led her back to the other side of the stoop. Caroline knew that Martha wanted to watch the game of checkers as much as she did, and she was just about to say so when Mr. Carpenter laid his hand on her shoulder and said, "I'll bet you a penny that Lake wins fair and square, Caroline, and I'm afraid I need to get the missus her medicine soon as your mother's taken care of her business. So let's be on our way."

Caroline didn't have a penny, and she'd only heard about betting once before when Mother had warned Joseph and Henry it was a sin. Pertly, she responded, "Mother wouldn't want me to bet, Mr. Ben," and followed her neighbor across the stoop just as Mother walked out the door, holding Thomas with one hand and carrying a burlap sack in the other.

"I went as fast as I could," Mother greeted them. "Mr. Porter's waiting at the counter, Benjamin. He has the medicine all ready for you."

Mr. Carpenter saluted and hurried into the store.

"You! You!" A deep, furious voice burst forth from behind Caroline. Heart pounding, she spun around, her breath caught in her throat. At the foot of the stoop, an Indian stood glaring at the men who had gathered around the table. His head was shaved clean except for a narrow stripe of bristly black hair that cut across his gleaming scalp. Bold scarlet-and-white streaks were painted across his cheeks, arms, and bare chest, and Caroline could clearly see the rage in the man's piercing black eyes.

"Goodness glory!" Mother whispered frantically. Dropping the burlap sack, she swiftly pulled Thomas into her arms. "Martha, take

Eliza! Caroline, give me your hand. We must go! And no commotion, any of you!"

Without looking at Mother and the children, the Indian stepped up to the table. Shaking his fists, he shouted at Mr. Carleton, "You! Kill! Murder brother of Black Horse!" Whipping a thin silver knife out of his boot, the Indian held the flashing blade up against Mr. Carleton's neck.

Caroline turned and buried her face in Mother's skirt as Mr. Carleton responded in a voice shaking with fear, "I didn't do it! I didn't kill anybody."

Trying her best to be quiet, Caroline took Mother's hand. Then she heard the door to the general store open and Mr. Carpenter's clear, firm voice say, "Go now, Charlotte. And don't hurry. I'll be with you in a minute."

Peering up from behind Mother's skirt, Caroline watched as Mr. Carpenter handed Mother her burlap sack and walked confidently across the stoop. Dropping the bottle of medicine into his pocket, he raised his open hands in the air. "There must be some misunderstanding here," he was saying calmly. "Carleton can't even beat a man at checkers. How could he take someone's life?"

Mother's firm hand quickly guided Caroline and the rest of the children off the stoop and down onto the side of the road. The town had grown eerily quiet as passersby stopped to watch the drama unfolding in front of the general store.

Once the Quiners had crossed the road and were at a safe distance to wait for Mr. Carpenter, Caroline looked back and saw him talking and gesturing to the Indian. After a moment, the painted man jumped onto a sleek black mare and galloped off down the road. Soon Caroline could no longer see the man or his horse on the horizon. He had disappeared as quickly as he had appeared.

"The good Lord spare you, Benjamin! Taking such a risk!" Mother admonished her friend as they headed away from the crossroads of town.

"No risk there, Charlotte." Mr. Carpenter shrugged. "One lone man can't stand up against a whole pack of townsfolk, no matter how crazed with anger he is. Truth be told, I was more worried for the Indian than for Carleton."

"Did he hurt Mr. Carleton?" Caroline asked. Her heart was still pounding, and she had never before felt so frightened and confused. Father had had many friends who were Indians, and though she often didn't understand what they said, they had always been kind to her. Just last winter when her family hadn't eaten meat for months, two Indians had dragged a whole buck into their house, leaving them enough venison to last through spring.

"No, little Brownbraid," Mr. Carpenter said soothingly. "Carleton's fine."

"Mr. Ben saved his life! Right in front of our eyes!" Martha exclaimed, her eyes shining with admiration.

"Didn't do anything of the sort!" Mr. Carpenter's laugh rang loud. "That poor Indian didn't understand one word I was saying. He may have backed down this morning, but he was all painted up like he was ready for war, and I'd bet every penny in my pocket this town hasn't seen the last of him. Someone's killed his brother. Someone's bound to pay."

"That's enough talk about Indians," Mother said firmly. Her face was pale, and her grip on Caroline's shoulder hadn't yet relaxed.

"You're right, of course, Charlotte," Mr. Carpenter agreed. "Come on up here, young Thomas," he said, and swung the toddler up on his shoulders. "We need to walk faster than a jackrabbit if old Mr. Ben's going to get this tonic home 'fore dinner!"

On the way home, Mr. Carpenter whistled as many lively tunes as he could remember. Then he burst into a song that Caroline had never before heard.

"Old Dan Tucker was a fine old man,
He washed his face in the frying pan,
He combed his hair with a wagon wheel
And died of the toothache in his heel.
Git out the way for Old Dan Tucker!
He's too late to git his supper.
Supper's over and dishes washed,
Nothing left but a piece of squash!"

Caroline laughed out loud as Mr. Carpenter sang the silly words. Her spirits swelled along with Mr. Carpenter's deep voice, and finally, forgetting all about the trouble in town, she clapped joyfully and began marching along as her neighbor launched into another verse:

> *"I come to town the other night,*
> *I hear the noise and saw the fight;*
> *The watchman was arunnin' roun'*
> *Crying, 'Old Dan Tucker's come to town.'*
> *Git out the way for old Dan Tucker!*
> *He's too late to git his supp—"*

"Perhaps another song, Mr. Carpenter?" Mother interrupted hopefully.

"Right again!" Mr. Carpenter shrugged and quickly switched tunes.

> *"Oh, Charley he's a fine young man,*
> *Oh, Charley he's a dandy!*
> *Charley likes to kiss the girls*
> *And he can do it handy!*
> *I don't want none of your weevily wheat,*

I don't want none of your barley,
I want fine flour in half an hour,
To bake a cake for Charley!"

Martha giggled and clapped, and Eliza joined right in. But Caroline couldn't stop thinking about Old Dan Tucker coming to town, bringing noise and fights. Maybe the Indian with the painted face who called himself Black Horse was really Old Dan Tucker. If he ever came to town again, Caroline hoped she'd be far out of his way.

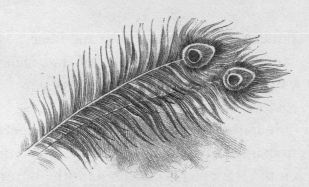

Peacock Feathers

Mother, Grandma, and the girls spent long days and evenings pickling and preserving. Each morning and afternoon, Caroline and Martha brushed clumps of dirt from fresh cucumbers, onions, and beans, wiped their outer skins clean, and handed them to Mother and Grandma. Once Mother and Grandma finished slicing the vegetables, Caroline and Martha packed the juicy chunks into wooden barrels. When each barrel was piled high, Mother poured in a mixture of vinegar, water, salt, and spices. The sharp brine stung Caroline's nose and lingered in the frame house long after Joseph and Henry had carried the tightly sealed barrels down to the root cellar.

It took a whole week and the sweet smell from a pot of apple preserves Mother simmered on the stove to rid the house of the bitter scent of the brine. Crocks and jars lined the long wooden table in front of the hearth, waiting to be filled with the hot fruit preserves. Caroline and Martha sat at the table, cutting squares of waxed brown paper to fit over the containers once they were filled. Mother had already used most of the mutton fat she had in the house to seal the blackberry preserves she'd made last month. Though it didn't seal the fruit as well, or keep the preserves as fresh as the mutton fat did, the waxed brown paper was a good substitute, and Caroline and Martha were very careful to cut their squares without wasting any paper.

"Charlie's just come by with word that his mother's fever's broke for good," Joseph burst into the house and told Mother. "He says she wanted you to be the first to know that she's finally on the mend."

"Thank heavens," Mother said with relief. "The poor thing suffered bouts of fever for over two weeks!" Stirring the simmering fruit with vigorous strokes, she added, "Living as we are, surrounded by all these swamps and lowlands, it's a wonder we all haven't caught the chill fever. Had Father and I known what the swamps would bring us, we surely would never have settled so close to them."

"Is Charlie still here?" Martha asked Joseph as soon as Mother had finished speaking. "Perhaps we could give him some preserves to take to Mrs. Carpenter. The apples are nearly finished cooking, aren't they, Mother?"

"Why, yes, Martha," Mother replied.

"It makes no difference," Joseph said. "Charlie left soon as he told us the news. And Hog's run off into the woods again, Mother. Henry and I are going to find him. I s'pect we'll be back before supper."

"Where are Thomas and Eliza?" Mother asked.

"They're out playing by the woodpile," Joseph answered.

"Not alone?" Mother asked sharply.

"Oh, no," Joseph replied quickly. "Henry's working right next to them, practically."

"Send the children inside before you leave, please, Joseph," Mother directed. "And be careful in those woods."

"Yes, ma'am." Joseph nodded, closing the door behind him.

Caroline looked questioningly at Martha. "Do you s'pose she's still worried on account of Old Dan Tucker?" she whispered.

"Who?" Martha whispered back.

"Old Dan Tucker. The Indian with the painted face!"

"Let's not even talk about *him*!" Martha shuddered. "It's too scary to think about."

Nodding, Caroline looked down at the brown paper she had been cutting. She hoped Mother would soon begin acting like herself again. Since the morning they had walked to the general store with Mr. Carpenter two weeks ago, Mother's words had been short, her demeanor quiet. She hadn't smiled or laughed much, and she had insisted on knowing the whereabouts of the children every time they left the house. Worst of all, she had stopped singing at night as she sewed in her rocker. She sat quietly now. Listening.

Caroline began cutting out another square, thinking back to the moment they had arrived at the frame house after their visit to the general store. Mother had pulled Joseph aside while Caroline and her sisters had washed up for dinner. In a far corner of the room, they had spoken quietly for several minutes, and Caroline could tell by Joseph's grave manner at dinner that Mother had told him about the trouble in town. After supper that night, while the girls embroidered their samplers and Grandma knitted, Joseph took the rifle down from its hook above the door and set it on the table. Under Mother's watchful eye, he carefully cleaned and loaded it.

Caroline couldn't help looking over at the door every few minutes that night. She half expected it to be flung open by the Indian.

It had taken her five restless nights before she finally stopped dreaming about the man's raging eyes, the bold red-and-white streaks painted across his face, and his angry shouts.

"It's ready now, I think," Mother called out as she peered into the steaming pot. "Please bring me the crocks one at a time."

Caroline and Martha took turns carrying empty crocks to the stove. Wrapping an old rag around the bottom of each crock, Mother carefully poured three ladlefuls of the steaming golden preserves into each one. "Now don't burn yourself," she instructed Caroline, handing her a full crock to carry back to the table. "Keep your fingers around the rag."

Being extra careful not to spill any hot preserves, Caroline walked so slowly that the heat of the clay crock burned her clear through the rags. "Ouch!" she cried out, setting it down in a hurry and blowing on her smarting fingers.

"You just have to walk faster, is all," Martha said as she stepped up beside Caroline and placed her container of preserves on the table.

"Perhaps you should carry the crocks to the

table, Martha," Mother suggested. "Caroline can start sealing them with the waxed paper, and I'll tie them with the twine once the preserves settle."

"Yes, ma'am." Caroline shook her sore fingers and happily agreed.

Centering a waxed-paper square over the top of the first crock, Caroline smoothed the paper down over the warm rim, pressing it down until it crinkled and tightly hugged the sides. The steaming preserves melted the wax and made it stick to the rim of the crock. When the first crock was finished, Caroline pushed it to the far end of the table and moved on to the next. She had just finished sealing her fifth crock when the door crashed open against the washstand.

As Caroline whirled around, Martha shrieked and flung her hands up to her mouth. The crock of hot preserves that she had been carrying smashed on the wooden plank floor, leaving a thick, syrupy puddle of apples and broken pieces of clay at her feet. The Indian with the painted face was in the kitchen.

"Be quiet, girls," Mother commanded. She moved next to Caroline and motioned Martha to her side.

Even if Caroline had wanted to move, she couldn't have. Stiff with fear, she stood very still and shut her eyes as tightly as she could.

"What is it you want?" Mother finally asked. Caroline could not believe how calmly she spoke.

The house remained silent until Caroline heard the soft padding of moccasined feet crossing the wooden floorboards. Heart pounding frantically, she opened her eyes and saw the Indian disappear into the parlor.

"Mother Quiner," Mother said in dismay. "We must go to her."

When Mother and the girls stepped into the doorway of the parlor, Grandma was still napping peacefully in the daybed. The man was nowhere near her. Instead, he was standing in front of a looking glass that was hanging on the wall across from the front door. A wooden shelf hung beside the mirror, a flowered glass vase set on top of it. One by one, the Indian pulled a handful of peacock feathers out of the vase and pushed them into the strip of braided hair that cut across the center of his scalp and fell down the back of his head past his shoulders.

When he had finished placing the last feather in his hair, the Indian stared at his reflection in the looking glass. The scarlet stripes of war paint hid his features, and though his black eyes were no longer flashing with anger and pain, the peacock feathers poking out of his braid gave him a wild and exotic look.

No longer interested in the parlor, the Indian turned abruptly and headed back into the front room, Mother and the girls walking backward in front of him. Examining the sewing table first, he picked up a thimble, a spool of thread, and Grandma's crochet needles. Then he reached for Caroline's sampler, and she held her breath as he turned it every which way before finally setting it back on the table. Deciding to take the thimble and spool of thread, he then headed off to search the dish dresser. Not finding anything of interest there, the Indian moved onto the table and leaned over a steaming crock of preserves. Smelling it once, he cautiously dipped two fingers into the sticky mixture and licked his fingertips. Then he turned to the shelves on the far side of the room where Mother kept her staples. He knelt down and was about to open a sack of flour when Henry came barreling into the room through the kitchen door, Joseph close on his heels.

"We found Hog!" Henry cried. "Let's eat!"

"We have a guest," Mother said as the Indian stood up and stared at Joseph and Henry.

Caroline watched the color drain out of her brothers' faces. Joseph glanced at the rifle above the door, but his eyes met Mother's and he silently stood his ground.

"Man!" the Indian said unexpectedly.

"What man?" Mother asked.

"Man of house!" he answered.

"There is no man here," Mother answered. "Only my boys."

The Indian walked over to Henry and Joseph

and stood in front of them, arms folded across his chest. He nodded his head and pointed at Henry. "Brother?" he asked, staring at Joseph.

"Yes," Joseph answered.

Turning back to the table, the Indian picked up the crock of preserves he had tasted and left the house without another word, the peacock feathers in his hair fluttering with each step.

"Thomas and Eliza!" Mother shouted the moment the man was gone. "They never came inside!"

"I bet they're still out by the woodpile," Joseph said, running for the door.

Caroline and Martha followed Henry, Joseph, and Mother into the chilly fall air. Together, they raced to the woodpile. "They were playing right here just a few minutes ago when we went after Hog!" Joseph said frantically. Thomas and Eliza were now nowhere to be found.

"I told you to send the children into the house before you left," Mother cried, her voice rising. "There's no telling what he's done with them!"

"It's my fault, Mother," Joseph said immediately. "I'll search the barn. Henry, take Wolf and go out back toward the creek. They may have tried to follow us to the woods without our knowing."

"Mama?" Eliza called out fearfully as she dashed from the side of the house all the way across the yard and straight into Mother's arms.

"Thank goodness you're safe!" Mother cried, hugging Eliza tightly. "Where's your brother, Eliza? Do you know where Thomas went?"

"No." Eliza shook her head, tears spilling down her cheeks. "I saw the man and I ran away. . . ."

"Did Thomas run too?" Mother asked, trying to keep her voice steady.

"I didn't see him," Eliza sobbed. "He was gone before—"

"Martha, Caroline, look in the garden while I take Eliza back into the house to sit with Grandma," Mother ordered.

"Yes, ma'am," Martha said. Caroline wanted to answer, but her voice was stuck in her throat. Brushing away tears, she ran as fast as she could toward the garden.

"You look here. I'll go look on the other side," Martha said, and ran off without waiting for a reply. Hurrying past the many rows of vegetables, Caroline quickly searched through crisp, drying leaves and vines. Passing by a cluster of round orange pumpkins, she hoped to see little Thomas dragging one of the large gourds by its curly gray handle, but he wasn't there. Finally reaching the corn, she frantically ran up one row and down another, leaving the dried-up ears and crunchy yellow-brown leaves rustling and swaying behind her as she passed.

Caroline burst out from beneath the tall stalks of corn that surrounded her like a dense forest of bony trees. Standing still, she listened carefully, straining to hear a joyful shout that her little brother had been found. The sun filtered down through the cornstalks' bristly fringe, warming her head and splashing light around the cool earth beneath her feet. Except for the gentle hum of the breeze, though, and the light crackling of the dry leaves, Caroline didn't hear a sound.

"Look! Corn!" A sweet, happy voice burst into giggles from behind Caroline, and she spun around to find Thomas's face glowing up at her.

"Thomas!" Caroline cried. Throwing her arms around her little brother, she squeezed him so tightly that he whimpered and tried to wiggle his way out of her grip.

"Funny corn!" Thomas said, raising an ear full of gold, orange, and wine-colored kernels high above his head.

"Leave the corn here. We must go find Mother," Caroline said, grasping her little brother's chubby hand tightly and leading him out of the garden. "She's going to be so happy to see you!"

Mother cried and laughed and hugged Thomas a dozen times before scolding him soundly for wandering off into the garden alone. Caroline received a second round of

114

hugs and praise, and then Mother hugged Henry, Martha, and Joseph as well.

"Do you think that Indian will ever come back?" Henry asked as the girls washed up for supper and cleared the table.

"I don't believe so," Mother answered, her voice full of cheer. "He knows he won't find what he's looking for in this house."

Later that night, Caroline tied the laces of her nightcap and climbed into bed. Settling her head on her thick, soft pillow, she pulled the heavy quilt up to her chin. The cold autumn wind circling the frame house rattled the windowpanes and filled the room with a chilly draft that hinted of harsh winter weather to come. Caroline paid it no mind. Closing her eyes, she listened to Mother's sweet song drifting up to the rafters and was soon fast asleep.

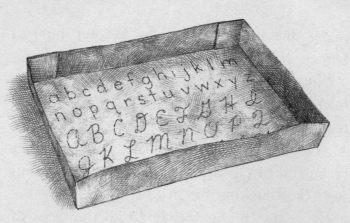

Grandma Says Good-bye

Before long, all traces of color had faded from the meadows, trees, and creek sides in Brookfield. Etched in gray and black and brown, the cold, dreary world stood silent, waiting for the first snowfall.

Watching a tangle of bare limbs on the oak tree outside her window shiver in the November wind, Caroline shivered too. It didn't matter that the sun was shining outside the windowpanes, or that her red flannels were snug and warm beneath her blue wool dress. Caroline felt cold and miserable. Tomorrow morning Grandma was going to Milwaukee. Tomorrow Grandma was saying good-bye.

Weeks before, Grandma had received a letter from Father's younger brother. Uncle Elisha's wife had suddenly taken ill. Uncle Elisha asked that Grandma come to Milwaukee and help care for his sons while he nursed his wife back to health and worked to keep his newspaper printing. As Caroline listened with a lump in her throat, Mother insisted that Grandma go to Milwaukee. "We've borrowed you long enough, Mother Quiner," Mother said. She was smiling at Grandma, but her eyes were full of sadness. "Elisha needs you now, and you must go to him. The children and I will manage fine, though we'll miss you terribly."

Caroline wanted to protest, but she didn't dare. She knew Mother would chide her, so she thought about Uncle Elisha instead. She didn't care for Father's brother, even though she had no reason to dislike him. It had been two years since she had seen her uncle. One gray afternoon he had arrived at their little frame house with Grandma and his sister, Aunt

Margaret, bringing news that Father's schooner had been lost at sea. Caroline hated to think about that terrible day, but she did remember how Uncle Elisha had kindly stayed in Brookfield and helped prepare the house and barn for the winter before returning home. Soft-spoken and funny, he had tried everything he could think of to cheer his nephews and nieces, telling wonderful stories about Father as often as he remembered one. Caroline had listened eagerly, relishing the tales. Every night she took her uncle's remembrances to bed with her, dreaming about Father and the many adventures he and his brother had shared as children.

After Uncle Elisha returned to Milwaukee, Grandma stayed on in Brookfield. Tonight, however, Uncle Elisha would arrive from Milwaukee once again, and tomorrow Grandma would go to live with him and Caroline's cousins, William, George Henry, and John. Caroline couldn't help wishing that Uncle Elisha would never visit again. Every time he came and went, she was left with an aching loneliness that took too long to go away.

Footsteps thumped up the stairs and Caroline turned to find Martha's dark eyes peering at her through the stair railing. "Mother says come down now," Martha said. "She says we must spend all the time we can with Grandma, seeing how she's leaving tomorrow."

Caroline looked back at the oak tree and the crooked, black limbs shuddering in the wind.

"What are you doing?" Martha asked. Climbing the last two steps, she passed the beds and the curtain that divided the room to look out the window. "What are you looking at, anyway?"

"Nothing," Caroline replied glumly.

"Then come downstairs," Martha said. "Don't you want to be with Grandma before she goes away?"

"Henry and Joseph are with her," Caroline said. "And you and Eliza and Thomas. She's got plenty of folks to visit with, far as I can tell."

"Well, if I were you, I'd rather be downstairs with Grandma than up here all by myself looking out at nothing but some old frozen tree!

119

That's just plain silly!" Martha exclaimed. Starting toward the stairs, Martha turned back suddenly, her voice soft. "I'm going to miss her too, you know. I'm just not as quiet about it as you." With a whirl of her brown woolen skirt, Martha was off, braids and bows flouncing about as she went down the stairs.

Mother appeared a few moments later. "What's keeping you, Caroline?" she asked. "I expect you to come downstairs this minute."

Head bowed, Caroline sighed, "Yes, ma'am." Then she took a deep breath, shivering again as she crossed the cold, drafty floorboards to the stairs.

"Whatever is wrong?" Mother asked, lifting Caroline's chin.

Caroline tried not to cry in front of Mother, but she just couldn't help it. Tears spilled down her cheeks as she began, "I wish, I wish . . ."

Mother pulled Caroline close against her. Her black woolen dress was rough and scratchy, but Caroline didn't mind. She wished she could hold on to Mother forever.

"I wish Grandma could stay with us too, but Uncle Elisha needs her now," Mother whispered in her ear. Reaching into her pocket, she pulled out a corner of her handkerchief and dried Caroline's tears. "Milwaukee isn't so far away. We'll see Grandma again come spring."

"We will?" Caroline asked hopefully.

"The good Lord willing," Mother promised. "Now we must get downstairs. Grandma is waiting for you."

Caroline followed Mother down the stairs. Grandma was rocking slowly in front of the hearth, Henry, Martha, and Eliza seated at her feet. Thomas bounced lightly on her knee, and Joseph leaned against the far side of the hearth. Grandma was telling one of her stories, and the whole room was still, listening. Even the fire blazing in the hearth seemed to sizzle and snap more quietly as if to hear every word.

"There you are, my dear." Grandma paused and greeted Caroline. "Come and sit."

Henry moved over and Caroline sat down beside him, smoothing her dress over her crossed legs. "You didn't miss anything yet," Henry informed her. "Father's five years old in this story, and he's decided he wants to shoot his first deer."

"Day and night your father talked about getting his first buck, and begged his papa to take him along on the first hunt of the winter. Your grandfather finally agreed," Grandma continued. "That morning dawned bright and cold, and Henry was up 'fore anybody, so full of excitement you'd think he'd about burst. I tucked his scarf all around his neck, ears, and cheeks and helped him into his boots and coat. Then I sent him on his way with your grandfather, expecting to see them back 'fore supper. Well, early in the afternoon, just after dinner, Henry slipped in through the door, his cheeks two red dots, his hair all mussed up, his boots full of snow and ice."

"What happened to him, Grandma?" Martha straightened up on her knees and asked.

"I asked exactly that, Martha. I said, 'What's

happened to you, Henry? Where have you been? And where's your father?'"

"What did he say?" Caroline asked.

"He said, 'Papa went off scouting and told me to be real quiet while I was waiting for him. Said deer could be walking by 'most anytime. Sure enough a whole herd came through the trees, and I didn't have anything to shoot 'em with, and I couldn't yell for Papa,'" Grandma continued in a voice that sounded like five-year-old Father's. "'So I started real slow, backing away and thinking I could get out of sight and find Papa without scaring off the deer. I walked two or three steps, Mama,' he said, 'then all of a sudden I couldn't move. I was stuck to something and I couldn't go anywhere.'"

"What'd he get stuck to?" Henry jumped in as Grandma paused to take a breath.

"A corner of his scarf had come undone and fastened itself to a tree branch behind him." Grandma smiled, her skin crinkling all around her bright eyes. "He pulled and tugged at that scarf, but it wouldn't come lose. I had tucked it around him so tight, he was stuck but good.

Your father stood fastened to that tree for a long time, still he never hollered or made a fuss because he didn't want to scare off the deer."

"Did Grandpa find him?" Joseph asked. He was standing straight up now, his arms folded across his chest.

"No, one of the deer found him first," Grandma replied.

"A deer!" Caroline cried.

"Your father heard some rustling in the trees and turned to find two soft brown eyes staring down at him. Seems a yearling had happened upon the scene and was quietly watching him. Your father remained still and silent, and for a time they just looked at each other. The deer was soon joined by others, and Henry got to thinking that if he didn't get away soon, some hunter would aim and shoot at the pack of deer, not knowing a little boy was stuck to a tree right in the center of the herd. In a panic, your father finally tore through the yarn on one side of his scarf, wriggled out of it, and ran off through the woods fast as he could. The deer fled in the opposite direction with a scrap of Henry's scarf trailing from one antler. And the rest of the herd that Henry'd been so careful not to frighten fled right along with him."

"How did the scrap of scarf get on the deer's antler?" Joseph asked.

"Your father never could figure!" Grandma chuckled.

"Did he find Grandpa?" Martha asked excitedly.

"No, he had lost his scarf and scared off half a dozen deer," Grandma explained. "He knew he was in a load of trouble. So instead of looking for Grandpa, Henry decided to go back and retrieve his scarf."

"Did he find it, Grandma?" Caroline asked.

"No, but he came up behind his papa an hour or so later. Grandpa's gun was cocked and ready to shoot. Henry didn't call any attention to himself. Instead, he looked to see what your grandpa was aiming at. Lord save me if it wasn't the very same deer that had run off with part of Henry's scarf."

"Grandpa shot it and Father got his scarf back!" Henry shouted triumphantly.

"No, young Henry," Grandma chuckled. "Your father, who was so eager to shoot his first deer just that morning, found your grandpa aiming at the deer that had been standing not five feet from him all the while his scarf was stuck to that tree. He suddenly couldn't bear to see the young thing killed. Knowing he didn't have time enough to run through the woods and scare the deer proper without your grandpa knowing, he decided to scream and holler, and make enough noise to send all the living things in the forest scurrying away lickety-split!"

"Goodness glory!" Mother exclaimed. "Henry never told me this story, Mother Quiner. What did Father Quiner do when Henry was making all that noise?"

"Near jumped right out of his skin, to hear Henry tell it," Grandma answered. "Your grandfather was so stunned by all the hollering, he jerked his rifle up and shot at all the leaves and branches and sky above. Served

William right, I declared, taking such a little one off hunting like he was a grown-up."

"Did Father get a caning?" Henry asked.

"He ran off before your grandfather could catch him, and he hid out back of the house till after dinner, waiting for his papa to return. By the time he finally came in out of the ice and snow, Henry was frozen through and had decided that as bad as a caning might be, it was better than freezing to death. He told me the whole story, teeth chattering and all, and I kept him in front of the fire until your grandfather arrived with news that young Henry had disappeared. He was so relieved to see his boy in front of the hearth, he didn't think twice about missing that deer."

As the afternoon light faded into the soft glow of evening, Grandma told all the stories she remembered about Father. She spoke of him all through supper, and she talked while the dishes were washed and dried and put away. The sun had long since slipped into the night sky when she finally stopped telling stories and called Caroline over to the sewing table.

"There's one more bit of work we must do before I leave tomorrow, little one," Grandma said. Reaching under the table, she pulled out a small box and carefully began cutting off the sides. "There!" she said happily, holding the empty rectangle up for scrutiny. "As good a frame as any!"

"What's it for, Grandma?" Caroline asked curiously. Mother never cut her boxes; they were far too useful for storing goods.

"I've been thinking it's time we frame that sampler of yours, dear," Grandma answered. "I've sat by your side for months watching you complete every letter in the alphabet, and I can't bear to leave until I see your first piece of embroidery framed! Now get it right quick, Caroline, so Mother won't think I'm trying to keep you from your bedtime."

Caroline carefully pulled her sampler from the sewing box and glanced over all the letters that she had so carefully embroidered. At the top of the mesh, the lowercase letters of the alphabet were cross-stitched in a thin blue floss. The capital letters below had been running-stitched in a bright red scroll. Caroline's stitches weren't perfect, but it didn't matter. Her very first sampler was finished, and now it would be framed!

"Your stitches are lovely, Caroline!" Grandma smiled as Caroline shyly handed her the sampler. "Even that lazy-daisy stitch that gave you some trouble turned out just fine!"

Beaming with pleasure, Caroline watched as Grandma carefully smoothed the mesh on the table and set the box frame over it. "This frame will do until I can get you the wooden one that such a fine sampler deserves," Grandma told her as she skillfully attached the corners of the mesh to the corners of the box with a few deft stitches. The moment she finished, Grandma set her needle and thread on the sewing table and held the sampler up before her. "Why, it's perfect!" Grandma exclaimed. "Come, child!"

Caroline followed Grandma across the cozy room until they were standing in front of the hearth. The roaring fire made Caroline's cheeks tingle with heat, and illuminated the soft ivory linen in her sampler. Standing as tall as she could, Grandma reached up to the mantel and gently leaned Caroline's sampler against the gray stone hearth. There it stood proudly beside two wooden horses that Father had carved as a boy.

"Three of our most precious treasures in one place," Grandma said as she put her arm around Caroline and hugged her.

Caroline was still awake when Uncle Elisha arrived late that night. Turning her face into her pillow, she closed her eyes and tried to think about her sampler in its box frame, glowing in the firelight beside Father's horses. As she finally fell off to sleep, Caroline wished away the winter. Spring had to come soon, so she could be with Grandma again.

Christmas Trunk

Until Eliza crawled across the cold floorboards and tickled Thomas into a fit of giggles, the sparks snapping and flames hissing in the hearth were the only sounds railing against the frenzied wind howling outside the frame house.

"For shame, Eliza," Mother scolded. "Little ladies don't crawl across the floor, and they don't roughhouse, either. You may play with the wooden toys in the settle. Bring Thomas with you, please."

"Could you tell us again what Uncle Elisha's

letter said, please, Mother?" Caroline asked. Seated at the table with Joseph, Henry, and Martha for their afternoon lessons, she was supposed to be printing letters and words on her slate. But instead she was listening to the wind and wondering when she'd be able to see beyond the heavy layers of snow that were packed over each windowpane, shutting most of the daylight out of the house. Caroline couldn't wait to go outside, to breathe the cold air and feel the warm sunshine on her face. With each new day of heavy snowfall, she felt certain that the frame house was getting smaller and smaller.

"Uncle Elisha writes that Grandma has settled in just fine," Mother replied as she swiftly chopped turnips and potatoes at the far end of the table. "He said that his wife's health is slowly improving, and that he is very busy at the newspaper printing all the local news and keeping up on stories about the war with Mexico."

Joseph looked up from his reader, his eyes bright with excitement. "Does Uncle Elisha say how much longer we'll be at war, Mother?" he asked.

"I don't believe so," Mother said. She wiped her fingers on her apron and reached for the three sheets of paper on the table in front of her. "No, he doesn't mention the end of the war, Joseph," she answered, "but Elisha does say that his newspaper readership has grown by leaps and bounds since the war broke out, and that he's struggling to keep up with the demand for new stories about it. 'Folks here in Milwaukee are clamoring to read any and every report of battles and wartime events,' he writes. 'Some are proudly celebrating the victories of generals Scott and Taylor with considerable excitement, while others think the war's just President Polk's war, and a plot by Southerners to expand slavery.'" Putting away Uncle Elisha's letter, Mother reached for her knife and shook her head. "I imagine they're plenty fed up with the whole mess back East," she said.

"I wish I could go off to war," Joseph said determinedly.

"Well, I am happy you cannot," Mother replied. "We need you right here at the moment, Joseph."

"Can I go?" Henry asked, his brow raised hopefully.

"I believe you mean *may* I go," Mother corrected. "No, you may not, Henry-O, and that's enough talk about war. It's high time you recited your spelling words."

"*May* Martha recite them first?" Henry suggested mischievously. He quickly leaned over his speller, hiding his grin from Mother's eyes.

"I'm learning Bible verses now, Henry," Martha countered. "I don't have to spell any words today."

"And you, Caroline?" Mother asked. "What are you working on?"

"I am practicing my letters and words," she responded. But her slate told a different story. She had scratched out only two words with her slate pencil. For three days now, since a heavy snowfall and bitterly cold winds had kept the boys home from school, Henry and Joseph had spent their afternoons studying with Caroline and Martha. Caroline found it especially hard to concentrate on her lessons with her brothers at the table. She was much too busy listening to their conversations to pay proper attention to her work.

Mother glanced across the table at Caroline's slate. "Only two words, Caroline!" she exclaimed. "Why, I'd thought you'd have your entire slate filled by now!"

Cheeks flushed with embarrassment, Caroline looked down at the table. "Yes, ma'am," she replied. She hated to disappoint Mother, but it was even worse to get scolded in front of all her brothers and sisters.

"My goodness if every one of you isn't fiddling around with your studies today," Mother continued as she inspected her children's half-hearted sums and scribbles. "The snow's bound to stop tomorrow or the day after, boys, and you'll find yourselves far behind the rest of the students if you don't keep up with your lessons. As for you, Martha and Caroline, I don't think I've ever—"

A loud *thump*, *thump*, *THUMP!* interrupted

Mother, and all heads turned toward the door. "Who on earth could possibly be traveling through all this snow?" Mother asked as she quickly wiped her hands on her apron and headed for the door.

With a vigorous tug, Mother pulled the door open from the snow and ice holding it tightly closed. A gust of winter air and a whirling cloud of snow blew into the house with a tall, stocky man and a young girl whose tightly wrapped scarf hid everything but a pair of sparkling blue eyes and a brown curl.

"Anna!" Caroline sprang up and ran to the door to hug her friend. "It's Anna, Mother! And she's brought her papa along too!"

"Do come in and warm yourselves by the fire!" Mother exclaimed. "Whatever brings you here through such terrible weather?"

"Forgive us, ma'am," Mr. Short said quickly, "to come in like this, no word or warning 't all." Running his hand over his brown curls, he wiped away the melting snowflakes that were beginning to trickle down his brow. "Today Anna and me, we went to the general store," he explained. "The mail came and Anna heard a man say he had a trunk to deliver. A trunk for a family Quiner. Anna near leaped out of her boots, such an excitin' thing and all. She begged me, 'Papa, carry the trunk to the wagon and bring it to Caroline and her family.'"

"What in the world . . . ?" Mother asked incredulously. Mr. Short's thick Scottish burr was difficult to follow, but Mother had clearly understood every word. "Are you certain the man said it was for us?"

"I asked Mr. Porter." Anna's father nodded. "He said so too."

"Where could such a trunk have come from?" Mother wondered aloud.

Mr. Short shrugged. "I will carry it in and you will see, right?"

Speechless, Mother nodded. "Shall I send one of the boys out to help?" she finally asked, as Anna's father pulled the collar of his coat tightly against his neck and ears.

"No thank you, ma'am," Mr. Short said gruffly. "I can manage fine."

As soon as Mr. Short disappeared into the

snow, Mother turned to Anna. "Tell me, child," she said, "did the man who delivered the trunk say anything about where he brought it from? Did you see any markings or words on it, perhaps?"

"No, ma'am." Anna's eyes twinkled with excitement, and her smile stretched from one bright pink cheek to the other. "I heard that man talking to Mr. Porter, and I thought that if I had such a trunk waiting for me, I wouldn't want it sitting all alone in some store. I'd want to open it soon as I could. So I asked Papa to bring it here. I hope you don't mind, Mrs. Quiner."

"Mind? Why, of course not, Anna!" Mother hugged her. "You've done a very kind thing for all of us. If it hadn't been for you, that trunk would have been at the general store for days."

"Maybe Uncle Elisha and Grandma sent it!" Martha cried. During all the excitement, she and Henry and Joseph had jumped up from the table and were now standing eagerly by the door.

"I don't believe so," Mother mused. "He would certainly have mentioned it in his letter, and that came days ago."

"Maybe it's from some stranger we never saw before," Henry suggested. "Maybe it's a trunkful of Christmas surprises!"

"Henry-O! How your imagination does run away with you." Mother laughed. "The trunk may indeed be for Christmas. And it is more likely that someone we know sent it. But who?"

"Christmas!" Caroline clapped, and Martha spun around at the same time. Caroline had to hold back a shout of joy. First Anna had appeared out of nowhere with her father and the surprise trunk, and now it was almost Christmas! That most wonderful day always came soon after her birthday, and Caroline had turned seven years old just one week ago. Christmas must be coming soon, and the trunk must be full of Christmas surprises!

"Maybe it came from Boston," Joseph said. "Maybe Grandma and Grandpa Tucker sent it."

"They'd send a letter, perhaps." Mother

shook her head, her eyes still curious. "But a trunk? My folks have never sent a trunk before. I'm afraid we'll just have to wait and see."

There was a soft bump at the door, and Mother quickly pulled it open. Mr. Short stepped out of the blowing snow and Joseph leaped forward to help him carry the trunk.

"Careful, boy," Mr. Short warned. "The snow's made it awful slippery."

"Yes, sir," Joseph said. He grasped one side of the trunk, and step by step they slid it across the floorboards, leaving a sloppy trail of snow and ice from the door to the hearth.

"Will you be staying for supper?" Mother asked as she mopped up the wet floor.

"Thank you, but no, ma'am," Mr. Short said, rubbing his hands together and then wiping them on his coat. "Come, Anna. We must go now."

"But Papa!" Anna cried in dismay. "Can't we stay to see what's inside? Oh, please, Papa!"

"Anna, you and your father have come so far

out of your way already," Mother said gently. "And your mother will surely be keeping supper. If your father says you must go now, you must go."

Caroline longed for Anna to stay, but she knew from the tone in Mother's voice that it was time for her friend to go home with her father. "I'll tell you what we find in the trunk, Anna, every last thing. I promise," she whispered.

Anna's sparkling blue eyes filled with tears. "But . . ." she began.

"The child's mother is no longer living, ma'am," Mr. Short interrupted brusquely. "Anna and me lost her three years back."

Her throat suddenly tight, and her eyes beginning to burn, Caroline turned to her friend. She had always wondered why Anna's mother was never with Anna and her father. Impulsively, she grabbed Anna's hand and gave it a warm squeeze.

Mother caught her breath. "Oh, I am so sorry!" she said, smiling kindly at Anna and

Mr. Short. "Surely then, you and Anna must stay and sup with us this evening, Mr. Short. We have a pork stew left from dinner, and it won't take but a minute for me to add some more vegetables."

"Don't want to be no trouble, ma'am," Mr. Short said quickly.

"No trouble at all," Mother assured him. "We'd love to have your company; but I must warn you, we're fresh out of coffee. I'll oven-roast some barley and make it into a toddy that will warm us just fine. Now take off your coats and boots and leave them beside the door while I find an old rag to wipe off this trunk before it soaks the floor any worse."

"We don't have to wait until after supper to find out what's in this trunk, do we, Mother?" Henry asked woefully.

"Of course not, Henry." Mother laughed. "For once, I can't wait any longer than you!"

By the time Mother had finished wiping all the snow and ice off the heavy wooden trunk, everyone in the room was clustered around her, waiting impatiently to see what treasure it held.

Expertly jamming an iron poker beneath the rim, Mr. Short opened the trunk without scraping or cracking the wood. Mother slowly lifted the lid, while Caroline and Anna, Eliza and Martha, and Henry and Joseph leaned forward to peer inside. Only Thomas was unconcerned.

Fingers shaking with excitement, Mother reached in and picked up the note placed on the small stack of magazines at the top of the trunk. "It *is* from Boston," she said as she unfolded the letter. " 'Greetings to you, dear Charlotte, and the children,' " she read aloud. " 'And gifts to all of you from all of us. May the Lord bless you this Christmas. Mama.' "

Wiping the corners of her eyes, Mother folded the note and tucked it safely inside her apron pocket. Then she began picking up the magazines one by one. "Here's a *Godey's Lady's Book*, and two copies of *Saturday Evening Post*," she said, "a copy of *Home Journal* and *The Christian World*. I've never seen either of these before. Look, children! Here are three copies of *Youth's Companion*. Grandma's sent you your very own magazines too!" Pausing for a moment, Mother turned to look at the children, her eyes full of mischief. "Shall we stop here and wait until after supper to see what's underneath?"

"No!" six young voices shouted merrily.

"No, no, no!" Thomas mimicked.

Beneath the magazines, Mother discovered three books: *The Deerslayer*, by James Fenimore Cooper; *A Christmas Carol*, by Charles Dickens; and a small book of stories by Hans Christian Andersen. Beneath the books she found an assortment of small cans. "Why, I'll be if these aren't from S. S. Pierce!" she exclaimed.

"S. S. Pierce?" Martha asked. "Who's that?"

"A merchant from Boston," Mother explained. "I do believe there is food in these cans!"

Caroline had never before heard of food that came out of a can, and she watched closely, her eyes growing rounder and rounder as Mother lifted each item from the trunk. "Here are some Boston baked beans, and a can of cranberries. Goodness glory! They've even sent a can with Boston brown bread inside!" Mother turned the can over and over, studying it from top to bottom. "Is it possible someone's baked the bread in the can and sealed it?" she asked in awe.

"How do you get those cans open?" Joseph wondered aloud.

"I don't rightly know," Mother admitted.

"What else is in there?" Henry urged.

"Patience, Henry-O," Mother said. "We must enjoy every single item!"

With the greatest care, Mother pulled small packages of olives and capers and dried codfish from the trunk, along with jars of currant jelly, pickled cauliflower, ginger, and macaroni, and a small box of tea. "We won't have to worry about oven-roasting the barley now." She laughed, showing the tea leaves to Anna's father.

"It's like someone sent us a whole general store in a trunk!" Caroline exclaimed as Mother again reached into the wide wooden box.

"I wish Papa and I could get such a treasure!" Anna said softly.

"Why, I never!" Mother exclaimed. Pulling out a bolt of red gingham, a bolt of wool dyed a rich navy blue, and a bolt of gold silk brocade, she ran her fingertips softly over the brand-new material. "I'm certain there's enough here for all of us, if I use it well," Mother said, and Caroline could tell by the thoughtful look in Mother's eyes that she was already planning the dresses and shirts and trousers she'd soon be cutting out and sewing.

"Could I have a dress made from the pretty shiny material, Mother?" Caroline asked.

"Me too!" Eliza said.

"This material is far too expensive and impractical even for a church dress, girls," Mother said, her gaze resting on the bolt of gold silk brocade. "I shall put it away somewhere safe, and wait for an extra-special occasion to use it."

At the bottom of the trunk Mother found a special gift for the boys: a small checkerboard accompanied by two packs of checkers. "This is some pumpkins!" Henry shouted, gleefully snatching the pack of red checkers before Joseph had a chance to. "Let's play, Joseph!"

"You may play after supper," Mother said firmly. Reaching far down into the trunk, she pulled out the last items, three pairs of girls' shoes, each a different size. The shoes had been worn, but were made of fine brown leather that wasn't scratched or stained or worn through. Caroline stared at those shoes and hoped with all her might that one pair would fit her just right.

"You're so lucky," Anna breathed. Caroline only nodded her response.

Soon after supper, as the frosty white glow of daylight disappeared outside the window-panes and night fell, Caroline hugged Anna and said good-bye. Handing a can of Boston baked beans to Mr. Short, Mother thanked him again. "You've delivered all our Christmas surprises, and it isn't even Christmas yet!" She laughed.

With a final good-bye to Anna and her father,

Mother shut the door against the blowing snow and wind. Wrapping her shawl more snugly about her shoulders, she sat in the rocker and reached for one of the books she had pulled from the trunk earlier that afternoon.

Joseph and Henry quietly jumped each other's checkers. Martha sat at Mother's feet, a dozing Thomas curled up on her lap. Caroline took Eliza's hand and together they sat on the other side of Mother's rocker, beside the blazing heat from the fire.

" 'The Little Mermaid, by Hans Christian Andersen,' " Mother began.

" 'Far out in the ocean the water is as blue as the petals of the loveliest cornflower, and as clear as the purest glass. But it is very deep too. . . . Many, many steeples would have to be stacked one on top of another to reach from the bottom to the surface of the sea. It is down there that the sea folk live.' "

"What's a ocean?" Eliza interrupted.

"Miles and miles of blue water and waves as far as your eye can see, Eliza. An ocean is even bigger than a lake or a river," Mother replied.

"Is there an ocean in Boston, Mother?" Martha asked.

"Yes, Martha," Mother answered. "The Atlantic Ocean."

"And people live there?" Caroline asked.

"In this story they do." Mother nodded.

"I wish I could see the ocean," Martha said wistfully.

Leaning against her little sister, Caroline thought about those sea people living in the deep, lovely ocean. She wished she could see it too someday. And she wished with all her heart she could see the place called Boston where Mother had lived, the place where all the wonderful treasures in the Christmas trunk had journeyed from. But not now. At this very moment, with the fire warming her back, and the wind shrieking outside the snow-covered windowpanes, Caroline couldn't imagine any place she'd rather be than snug inside her little frame house.

January Thaw

Lying so close to Eliza was making Caroline even more hot and uncomfortable. Tossing and turning, she wriggled to the edge of the straw mattress. Her nightgown felt limp and her hair was damp beneath her nightcap. Caroline kicked off the heavy quilt and opened her sleepy eyes.

The first rays of morning sunlight shone through the window, filling the room with a thin white haze that sparkled with flecks of floating dust. Caroline took a deep breath of the warm, moist air. At bedtime last night she had jumped under the covers before the cold in the room gave her the shivers right through her nightgown. This morning the cold had disappeared. Sitting straight up, Caroline wondered if she had gone to sleep in January and awakened in May.

Caroline climbed out of bed as quietly as she could so as not to awaken her sisters, and crept across the room. The icy draft that usually hovered above the floorboards, freezing bare ankles and feet, was gone, and the thick dusting of snow that had framed the glass windowpanes had all but melted. Tiny beads of water clung to the corners of each pane, slipping and sliding lazily to the bottom of the glass.

Pressing her nose against the window, Caroline looked out. The sky was a bold, endless blue. The trees were bare and black and wet, and the brown fields below them were dotted with gray mounds of snow that seemed to shrink right before Caroline's eyes.

"It's spring!" Caroline breathed. "Winter's gone! Spring is here!"

"Shush, silly!" Martha grumbled from the

far side of the bed. "Spring doesn't come in January!"

"But it must, Martha," Caroline disagreed. "Because here it is! Outside our window, clear as day!"

Pushing her cap backward until it slipped down to her shoulders, Martha sat up on her elbows. "It's awful hot in here," she said.

"I told you! Spring is here!" Caroline crowed. "Come see for yourself if you don't believe me!"

Martha tossed the covers to the foot of the mattress and joined Caroline at the window. "It can't be!" she exclaimed in wonder. "All that snow! Gone!"

"It seems we're having a January thaw, girls." Mother smiled at them through the railing. "Wake the others, now. Let's not waste a moment of this glorious day!"

Laughing with delight, Caroline and Martha awakened Eliza and their brothers and hurried them to the window.

"Why, I'll be washed and hung out to dry!" Joseph gasped.

"Zooks!" Henry shouted at the top of his lungs. "Let's get outside!"

Chattering merrily back and forth across the curtain that divided the room, the children quickly dressed and dashed down the stairs to wash up and eat breakfast.

Henry swallowed his first spoonful of cornmeal mush and looked at Mother. "Do we have to go to school today?" he ventured to ask.

"I think not, Henry," Mother replied, turning the spoon right side up in Thomas's chubby fist. "I can't remember a day so warm this early in the year. Seems a shame to be indoors for a minute of it. Just this once, your studies can wait until nightfall, children. But you must finish your morning chores before playing."

Since most of their chores were outside, Joseph and Henry ran out the door the moment breakfast was over. Caroline helped clear the table and was in such a hurry to dry the dishes and cups that Mother had to hand three damp plates back to her so she could finish wiping them. Together Caroline, Martha, and Eliza ran upstairs to fluff pillows and mattresses, tuck and smooth sheets and quilts, sweep the floors, and tidy the room. As soon as they finished, they bounded back downstairs to find Mother.

"We've finished our chores," Caroline sang out.

"All of them," Eliza said proudly.

"May we please go outside now?" Martha finished.

"You must wear your shoes, girls, and your shawls, too," Mother cautioned. "It may feel like a warm spring day, but there's still a chill in the air, and the ground will be cold and wet."

A cool breeze greeted Caroline as she stepped out of the frame house, ruffling the gray shawl she had wrapped around her shoulders and the green ribbon that was tied in a bright bow at the bottom of her braid. Closing her eyes and lifting her face to the sky, Caroline breathed in the refreshing air and grinned happily as warm sunlight spilled onto her face.

"Come on." Martha tugged at Caroline's sleeve. "Let's go get Joseph and Henry!"

Grabbing Eliza's hand, Caroline ran along beside Martha to the woodpile, the soggy earth sinking beneath her every step. Wolf pranced from side to side and barked happily as Caroline rushed over to him and patted his side.

"Soon as we finish splitting these last few logs and get them in the house, how 'bout a game of poison tag?" Henry shouted to his sisters as they raced up to the woodpile.

"Poison tag!" Caroline clapped. "I love that game!"

Martha immediately noticed that her brothers weren't wearing any coats or shoes. "Mother said we had to wear shoes and shawls, Henry and Joseph," she said.

"Then wear them," Henry said. "Mother didn't tell us any such thing!"

"Well, if you don't have to wear any shoes, then I'm not going to either!" Martha huffed. Untying her laces as quickly as she could, she pulled off her shoes and stockings and sank her bare toes into the wet soil. "It's so cold," she gulped, marching around in a small circle. "But your feet get used to it after a while, don't they?"

Caroline looked down at her shoes. She had been wearing them for only a month, since they had arrived in the Christmas trunk. Though they weren't brand-new, they looked and felt newer than any shoes she had ever worn, and they were much, much finer than Martha's hand-me-down shoes. Fashioned out of soft brown leather, the new shoes had laces that climbed all the way up Caroline's ankle. The moment she tried them on, Caroline knew they were too long and roomy for her, but she hadn't told Mother. Instead, she had promised herself that she'd keep this pair of shoes as clean and new as possible, since it would be a long time before her feet grew too big for them.

Don't forget to wear your shoes, girls. Mother's words rang in her ears. Lifting the hem of her dress, Caroline held her foot straight out in front of her, turning her shoe slowly from side to side. In just one short run from the house to the woodpile, the leather sides and tip of each toe had turned black with wetness. The sides and soles were clumped with sticky black dirt. Caroline decided. She carefully unlaced her shoes and peeled off her scratchy wool stockings. Shivers shot up and down her legs and spine as puddles of icy-cold water sprang up around her feet. "Ouch!" she gasped.

"Don't just stand there, little Brownbraid." Henry laughed. "Move around some!"

As Joseph and Henry swung their axes into logs and Wolf barked, Caroline and Martha danced and giggled and hopped all around the woodpile, trying to keep their feet from smarting in the cold, muddy soil. "I want to dance too!" Eliza shouted, and began pulling at her shoes.

An exuberant voice stopped Martha and Caroline in mid step. "Seems to me such fine dancing needs some fine music!

"Jim crack corn, but I don't care!
Jim crack corn, but I don't care!
Jim crack corn, but I don't care!
My master's gone away!"

"Charlie!" Martha exclaimed as Charlie Carpenter sang out the last line of the song and bowed dramatically.

"Don't stop dancing now!" he urged. His straight black hair hid his eyes, but his grin was perfectly visible. "I know the second verse too! Pa's just taught it to me. He says it's a brand-new song!"

"Hey, Charlie, get hold of the ax in the barn and help us with these logs," Henry called to his friend. "Then we can play us a game of poison tag!"

"I'd much rather do the singing than the swinging!" Charlie laughed out loud and stood straight up. "How about if I drag the split logs into the house instead?"

"Leave them in front of the woodpile, Charlie," Joseph directed. "I'll stack them later on. And you girls move away from here before one of these flying wood chips hurts you but good!"

"We could go down by the creek while we're waiting for them to play poison tag," Caroline suggested. "The grass is so wet, it'll make perfect dolls!"

Tugging at her lower lip, Martha hesitated. "We could stay and help carry the wood into the house," she suggested, "and then we'd be able to play even sooner!"

"I want to make grass dolls!" Eliza cried. "And I want to take my shoes off too!"

"We don't need more help now that Charlie's here, Martha," Joseph said. "We'll come out to the creek soon as we're finished. We can play tag there just as easy as here."

"But . . ." Martha began to protest, until Henry grinned wickedly and opened his mouth to speak. "All right! I'm going," she quickly said. "So you just be quiet, Henry Quiner."

"Come on, Wolf," Caroline called as the three girls raised their skirt hems up above their ankles and ran past the garden and barn.

"Why do you want to get all dirty carrying wood inside the house, Martha, instead of making dolls with us by the creek?" she asked on the way.

Martha shrugged. "I don't, really."

"Stop!" Eliza urged. "My shoes are cold, and they're hurting my feet!"

"Lean up against Caroline, Eliza," Martha ordered. "And give me one foot at a time."

Eliza did as she was told. The moment her feet were free, she shrieked happily and bounded off toward the creek. Tying Eliza's shoelaces together, Martha slung them over one shoulder. "We'd best not let her get too far ahead," she said.

Caroline, Martha, and Wolf followed Eliza across the soggy field until they came upon the creek. Sloshing and churning and sparkling merrily in the sunlight, the creek rushed along, seeping into the wetlands surrounding it.

"Wait here, Eliza—we'll get the grass," Martha said, and stepped into the mucky, ice-cold marsh beside the creek.

"It's just the right length for dolls!" Caroline

exclaimed. Lifting her skirt up to her knees, she waded in after Martha. "Stay here, Wolf," she ordered.

Wolf hung back from the marsh, panting softly as Eliza waited impatiently and her sisters yanked handfuls of tall grass from the marsh. When their arms were full, they dunked the grass into the icy water at their feet and pulled it out dripping wet. Holding their skirts up with one hand and the wet grass close against their shawls with the other, they trudged back to more solid ground, thick, heavy mud tugging at their ankles with every step.

Once they were on solid ground, Caroline swept her feet and toes across the wet grass, trying to wipe off all the dirt. Shaking a final mud chunk from her toe, she asked, "Where should we sit, Martha? The ground's still awful wet."

"Let's go a little bit farther away from the creek," Martha said. "We can take off our shawls and sit on them."

"But they'll get soaked!" Caroline exclaimed. "And full of dirt, too!"

"I expect they'll get wet," Martha agreed. "So we'll just set them out in the sun to dry while we're playing tag. They'll dry before dinner. As for getting dirty, I don't think so, Caroline. Snow is wet, but it's also clean and white. And the ground is wet with melted snow. So how could snow water get anything dirty?"

Reluctantly Caroline agreed. They found a drier spot and placed the grass they had collected in a pile. Pulling their shawls from their shoulders, they folded and laid them on the ground. "Sit, Wolf. And you too, Eliza. Here, next to me," Caroline said. "I'll help you make your doll."

Reaching for a handful of the wet, stringy grass, Caroline held one end tightly and ran her other hand across the shaft from end to end until all the blades of grass stuck together and all the edges were smooth. Then, looping the shaft over and lining up the ends, she said, "Hold this, Eliza, while I tie the neck."

Eliza held the grass loop still while Caroline tied a single thick blade of grass tightly around the top of the shaft, just below the loop. "There's the head!" Caroline said. Spreading out the grass from side to side in the little circle she'd just made, she quickly fashioned a perfectly round head. Then she fanned the two separate columns of grass below the head into one long trunk. "Now for the arms," she said, lifting a few blades of grass up from the left and right sides of the doll's body and tying them together at the tips with a single blade of grass. "And the waist," she continued, tying another blade of grass tightly about the middle of the doll, giving it a long grass skirt. "Perfect!" she exclaimed.

"Oh, Caroline"—Eliza clapped—"she's so pretty!"

"She needs a necklace," Caroline decided, taking the doll back from Eliza. "Go find some berries or seeds, or bits of pinecone, Eliza, so we can make necklaces. I'll make my doll while you're gone."

Caroline watched her little sister hurry away. "Look, Martha!" she cried. "Eliza's dress is wet clear through where she was sitting."

"She'll dry soon enough," Martha assured her.

Caroline suddenly noticed that her own skirt felt damp beneath her. Shifting to a drier spot on her shawl, she reached for another handful of grass. By the time Eliza returned with an apronful of wrinkled berries and seeds, three grass dolls were lying on the ground, waiting for their necklaces to be strung. Caroline had just found a pointy twig and was beginning to poke holes through the berries when Henry, Joseph, and Charlie thundered across the field.

"We're ready!" Henry cried. "Charlie's going to be It first, since he's visiting, all right?"

"Yes!" Martha exclaimed.

"Leave the berries here, Eliza," Caroline said, pointing to the spot where she had set down her stick. "We can make our necklaces after the game." Jumping up, she smoothed the back of her skirt and felt an icy-cold dampness against her legs. Her skirt was soaked.

"Look at you girls!" Joseph scolded. "You're

soaked to the skin. You'd best get in the house and take off those clothes before you all get sick."

"Who are you to say?" Martha answered defiantly. "I'm not one bit cold, and our dresses will dry just fine once we're running around in all this sunshine!"

"We won't have much of a game with only three players, Joseph," Henry pointed out. "I say let them play one game, at least."

"Are you too cold to play, Caroline?" Joseph asked, his dark-brown eyes looking straight into hers.

Caroline hadn't thought about being cold. The brilliant sun was casting a warm glow over the meadow, and though the steady breeze was brisk, it wasn't biting. But her feet and toes were tingling, and her skirt and petticoats were drenched and lying heavy and wet against her legs. Looking away from Joseph's eyes, Caroline answered, "I want to play."

"Well, don't say I didn't tell you!" Joseph shook his head. "You're It, Charlie."

"Spread out then, everybody," Charlie cried. "Ready, set, go!"

Shrieking and running as fast as they could, the rest of the players dashed around the clearing, trying to avoid Charlie and a leaping, barking Wolf. Gaining on Joseph, Charlie leaped after his friend, grabbed his shoulder, and shouted, "Surprise, Joseph! You're It!"

As Joseph began, "Ready, set . . ." Henry quickly interrupted. "This is *poison* tag, Joseph. You have to hold on to your shoulder where Charlie tagged you before you can go!"

"I know, I know." Joseph placed his hand on his shoulder and yelled, "Go!"

Caroline ran as fast as she could away from Joseph's pounding footsteps, but her heavy skirts slowed her down, and he grabbed her by the elbow in no time. "You're It, now," he laughed. "Hold on to that elbow!"

Giggling, Caroline held her elbow, shouted, "Ready, set, go!" and scampered after Henry, who led her around the field, running backward and scrunching up his nose and lips to make her laugh. Missing a dip in the ground ahead of him, Henry stumbled into a somersault right in front of Caroline. She lunged forward and caught Henry's bare foot just as he was trying to stand up and run. Tumbling over and over across the bumpy ground, Caroline finally came to a stop, gasping for breath and laughing up into the sun.

"How'm I s'posed to catch anybody hopping around on one foot?" Henry cried as he ran to help Caroline up.

"I got you fair and square!" Caroline insisted. Reaching for her brother's hand, she stood up and brushed off her skirt.

"No doubt about it," Henry said, "you're a terrible mess, little Brownbraid."

Looking down at her clothes, Caroline felt a lump growing in her throat. Dirt was smeared across her wet garments, and clumps of wet brown grass hung from her dress and apron.

"There's a whole bunch of dirt on your face too," Henry said.

Caroline rubbed the back of her dirty hand across her cold cheeks. "I hope I didn't ruin my ribbon," she said softly. Reaching behind her back, she gingerly pulled her long brown braid over her shoulder. Her precious green bow was not at the bottom. "Oh, Henry, it's gone," she whispered, trying not to cry.

"You're It, Henry, and you have to hang on to your foot," Charlie called out from down-field. "Quit stalling!"

Henry squeezed Caroline's shoulder. "I'll help you find it soon as I finish my turn," he promised.

While Henry hopped about the field, holding his foot with one hand and trying to grab at other players with his free hand, Caroline retraced her steps, with Wolf running along beside her. She looked everywhere she could think of to find her ribbon. It wasn't on the field where she had played poison tag. It wasn't beside the girls' shawls or the grass dolls and berries they had left lying on the ground near the creek. "Oh, Wolf, where could it be?" she fretted. Pausing in front of the muddy swamp beside the creek, Caroline shivered and decided she'd first search around the woodpile where she'd left her shoes and stockings. If her bow didn't turn up there, she'd ask Henry to help her look in the marsh itself.

Caroline ran back toward the house, her feet smarting and her teeth beginning to chatter. When she and Wolf arrived at the woodpile, she looked frantically for the log where she had left her things. Instead, she found Mother standing there, holding her shoes and stockings.

"Sakes alive," Mother said, her mouth straightening into a thin line. "Look at you, Caroline. I've never seen you such a mess!"

Caroline remained quiet. A hot tear rolled down her cheek.

"I've found the shoes and socks you are supposed to be wearing," Mother continued sharply. "Where is your shawl?"

"It's out back by the creek where we were making grass dolls," Caroline stammered.

"I suggest we get it immediately," Mother said. "Now march!"

Tears dripping from her cheeks and chin,

Caroline led Mother past the barn and the garden, Wolf lagging quietly a few steps behind. "Did you find it?" Henry shouted as Caroline and Mother passed through their game of poison tag.

Shaking her head back and forth, Caroline avoided her brother's eyes.

"So you've all misplaced your shoes and socks and shawls, I see," Mother said as she looked around the now-silent playing field. "Did I not tell you to wear your shoes and warm clothing?" she demanded.

"Not us," Henry answered honestly. Mother's furious glare silenced him immediately.

"Yes, ma'am," Martha whispered, looking nervously up at Mother. "But—"

"But nothing, Martha Quiner. You go and get your shawl and your sisters' shawls and get back to the house at once. Now!" Crossing the field swiftly, Mother swung Eliza up into her arms and began rubbing her red, shriveled feet. "Joseph Quiner," she snapped as she turned to her eldest son. "Eliza's feet are numb with cold. I expect *you* to know better, at the very least."

"I tried to tell them," Joseph began guiltily.

"Enough," Mother cut him off.

"I'm going to head home for dinner now," Charlie said. "Maybe we could finish the game later?"

"Not today," Mother said firmly. "Greet your parents for me please, Charlie."

"Yes, ma'am." With a wink to his friends, Charlie ran off without another word.

"I'm taking Eliza and Caroline back to the house now, boys," Mother said. "Fetch the rest of your things, put Wolf in the barn, leave your wet clothes by the hearth, and get up to bed. I'll send for you when your clothes are dry."

Martha caught up to her sisters and Mother as they were passing the garden. "Are the shawls as wet and dirty as the rest of you, Martha?" Mother asked her immediately.

Looking down at the grass, Martha replied, "Yes, ma'am."

"Leave them by the hearth with the rest of your clothes. You too, Caroline. And get upstairs under your quilt without another word."

Dismayed, Martha cried out, "We won't be able to play outside anymore?"

"I expect you'll spend dinnertime and most of the afternoon in your beds waiting for clean, dry clothes," Mother said.

"But it's a perfect day," Martha sulked. "Like spring! We could wear our Sunday dresses if we promise not to get them the least bit dirty. Please, Mother!"

Mother pulled open the door to the house. "Inside!" she ordered. "Get out of those clothes and up to bed."

Walking behind Martha, Caroline crossed the room to the hearth and watched Mother disappear into her room with Eliza. As she pulled her heavy wet dress over her head, words tumbled from her lips uncontrollably. "I should never have paid any attention to you when you took off your shoes and your shawl!" Caroline cried as fresh tears streamed down her cheeks. "You *always* have to do what

Joseph and Henry are doing! And Charlie too! I ruined my dress and my apron, *and* I have to stay in bed for the rest of the day. All because I listened to you!"

"It isn't my fault," Martha shot back angrily. "You didn't want to get your precious shoes all wet and dirty, and you know it, Caroline!" Rubbing her numb feet, she added halfheartedly, "Whoever would have thought that Mother would get so angry?"

Caroline dropped her head into her hands.

"What's wrong with you, anyway?" Martha snapped. "Stop crying. It's just a pair of shoes and a silly dress."

"I . . . I . . . lost my green bow," Caroline sobbed into her shaky hands. "It was my birthday present, and it was the prettiest bow I ever had."

"Oh," Martha said. "Well, if that's all it is, then don't waste any more worries. I found your bow under one of the grass dolls in the field, and I put it in my pocket. It wasn't dirty at all, far as I could tell." Martha lifted her dress up from the floor and pulled the grass dolls out of one apron pocket and Caroline's crinkly green ribbon out of the other. "Here." She grinned, handing it to Caroline and reaching down into her pocket again.

Smiling through her tears, Caroline looked over every inch of her ribbon, finding only one tiny smudge of dirt. "Thank you," she said gratefully.

"I'm sorry if I got us in trouble," Martha said.

"Me too," Caroline answered quickly.

"Let's get upstairs now 'fore we freeze to death," Martha urged. "I'm so cold, I can hardly feel my toes."

"Me too," Caroline admitted.

Martha paused. "When Mother brings Eliza up to bed, don't tell her how cold we are. She'll only get more angry, I think."

"I won't," Caroline assured her big sister as she followed her up the stairs.

"We can make necklaces for our dolls while we're waiting for our clothes to dry," Martha said. "I saved all the berries and the twigs you found, and a couple long strings of grass, besides. Here," she said, opening her cupped hands and pouring half of her berry-and-pinecone mix into Caroline's hand. "They were all in my pocket. You can carry some too."

Caroline and her sisters and brothers spent the rest of the warm, sunny afternoon in their beds, waiting for their clothes to dry in front of the fire down below. The girls strung berry necklaces onto wispy blades of grass and slipped them over their dolls' heads, whispering and giggling back and forth across the curtain so quietly that Mother never heard anything from the upstairs room.

By the time Mother finally carried a pile of warm, dry dresses and aprons, trousers and shirts, socks, and stockings upstairs, daylight was fading outside the window and the room was growing cool and dim. Delighted to be free from their beds at last, the children dressed quickly and ran downstairs to the table for supper. As she bowed her head and listened to Mother give thanks for their food and the lovely warm day, Caroline quietly slid her hand behind her back and reached for the bottom of her braid. Rubbing the soft folds of her green bow between her fingers, she smiled across the table at Martha and silently added her own prayer of thanksgiving.

The Resting Place

"Thank you for fixing the heel so quickly, Mr. June," Mother said. "The shoes looked so new at Christmastime, I didn't imagine they'd lose a heel in the blink of an eye."

"Balderdash, Mrs. Quiner!" the shoemaker replied, pulling two heel pegs from between his thin lips and plunking them down on the bench beside him. "Didn't take but a peg or two, right here at the tip of the heel." He turned the shoe in his hands, carefully examining the sole. "Mmm," he finally said, smiling down at Caroline and revealing two rows of brown-and-gold teeth. "My guess is it was worn by a shuffler before you, child."

"A shuffler?" Caroline asked as the shoemaker handed her the shoe.

"No doubt about it," he nodded, rubbing his stubbly chin with his knuckles. "A pair of shoes with leather this new couldn't possibly have a heel fall off unless a shuffler's broke them in."

Perplexed, Caroline said, "I've never heard of a shuffler before, sir."

"You've surely known one or two, young lady," Mr. June assured her. He bent his knees and slowly walked across the tiny shop, scuffling the soles and heels of his shoes over the floorboards, *chhh, chhh, chhh, chhh.* " 'Pick up your feet! Save your shoes,' I always tell the shufflers. But they never listen!" he exclaimed, arms flailing. "Those heels have taken a beating, Mrs. Quiner, and truth be told, the soles could follow suit at any time."

"We'll surely keep an eye on them, won't we, Caroline?" Mother prompted.

"Yes, ma'am," Caroline agreed. Tilting her foot up, she studied the bottom of the shoe she had just finished lacing up her ankle. The leather sole didn't look as new as the rest of the shoe, and Caroline's heart sank as she ran her fingers across all the scuff marks and scratches.

"Henry or Joseph will bring the shirt and coat I've mended for you day after next, Mr. June," Mother said. "Come along, Caroline."

Placing a hand on Caroline's shoulder, she led her down the room's narrow aisle, which separated the shoemaker's bench and tool table from his bed, stove, and washbasin. "Joseph will surely be back from the general store by now. I hope he hasn't been waiting long in this terrible weather."

Mother tied and tucked Caroline's scarf around her head and neck while Caroline buttoned her coat. With a final thank-you and good-bye to the shoemaker, they stepped out of the shop. Joseph was hurrying toward them, snow swirling frantically around him.

"Mr. Porter gave me extra needles and

thread," Joseph called loudly above the wind, "and he sent along more shirts and trousers for mending."

"Fine." Mother nodded, pulling on her black woolen mittens. "Let's get back to the house now, before this storm gets any worse. I should never have had us venture out today, I fear. But the wind didn't seem half bad before dinner."

Icy snow whipped at Caroline's face, nipping her cheeks and stinging her eyes as she followed Mother and Joseph home. The prickly wool scarf that covered her nose and mouth grew damper with each frosty breath and began scratching the back of her neck. She longed to pull it off and toss it to the winds, but she didn't dare even loosen it in Mother's sight.

Feeling crosser with every passing moment, Caroline tried to find something interesting to look at so she wouldn't keep thinking about her shoes and her itches. But the blustering squalls wouldn't let her. The crossroads of town had suddenly been transformed into a swirling cloud of snow and flashing yellow lights that faded in and out of sight with each gust. The storekeeper's stoop was deserted, the tavern was quiet, the blacksmith's doors were shut tight. Only the heavy wooden sign hanging from rusty chains on Dr. Hatch's roof answered the wind's howls, creaking loudly and banging against the wooden house as the sign rocked in the storm.

Plodding through crusty layers of snow, Caroline cringed as chunks of ice found their way into the space between her woolen socks and her leather shoes. A cold dampness seeped into her socks, and the wet wool began to chafe her ankles. Caroline ducked her head against the wind, growing crosser and crosser and hoping that her heel wouldn't fall off or her soles wear out before she got home. When Mother and Joseph stopped abruptly, Caroline bumped headfirst into the folds of Mother's long gray coat. It was all she could do not to stamp her foot and cry out in dismay.

"Ouch!" she complained. "Why are we stopping?"

"Hush, child," Mother said firmly.

Holding her tongue, Caroline stepped to Mother's side and peered ahead through the blowing snow. Two figures were trudging down the road toward them. The taller figure held the reins of a thin brown horse. A leather harness stretched tightly over the horse's shoulders, and as the figures moved closer, Caroline could see the narrow travois that the horse dragged behind it. Two long poles, trailing at an angle from the horse's back down to the snowy ground, had strips of bark and straps of leather tautly woven around and between them to form a low bed. The foot of the travois rested just above the snow. Its poles left two thin trails following horseshoe prints as it bumped along the road.

The horse moved slowly past Caroline, and she stole a look at the travois. An old man lay there, covered in a blanket that was patched together with brown, gray and black furs. The man's thick white hair spilled over the poles of the travois. His brown face was etched with

183

deep wrinkles, and his black eyes stared blankly at the troubled sky.

"Are you in need of help?" Mother called out as the strangers passed.

Startled, the taller of the two lifted his head and turned to Mother. "We need no help," he answered. A heavy blanket was draped over the speaker's shoulders, covering him down to the knees of his cloth trousers. His hair was tightly wrapped in a pale-colored cloth that was twisted and folded high on top of his head, and his bushy black eyebrows and black eyes stood out boldly on his young face. When Caroline looked up at him from behind Mother's skirt, she quickly realized he was not a man, but a tall boy who was not much older than Joseph.

"*No-taw-kah!*" A woman's voice rose above the wind. "Ask where we are to go!"

"I will find it, Mother," the boy insisted.

"We near the end," the woman standing beside the boy said determinedly. "We must ask."

Leaning forward, Caroline gazed at the

woman. A fur robe was gathered close about her neck and shoulders, hiding all but her face and buckskin mittens. Her long black hair, speckled with snowflakes, disappeared beneath the dense black robe. The woman's drawn face and tired eyes belied the strength of her voice.

"What is it you need?" Mother asked again. "Perhaps we can help."

"We must find the place where boulders and firs stand watch by running water," she called out above the wind. "We have strayed from the path that has taken us there before. Do you know this place?"

Mother turned to Joseph. "Have you ever seen it, Joseph?" she asked.

Joseph nodded. "She could be talking about the creek that runs through the back of our land."

"But the boulders don't sit and watch our creek, Joseph. They sit right *in* it," Caroline chimed in from behind Mother.

"You're right," Joseph agreed. "Maybe she means the creek outside town that passes by the mill."

185

"Can you tell us something else about this place?" Mother asked quickly. "Is it close to town, or—"

"We must go," the woman interrupted Mother. "We have little time."

"Please! Wait!" Mother urged, pointing at the travois. "This man surely needs help. We have a doctor in this town. My son can take you to him."

The woman stepped toward Mother, brushing loose, blowing strands of black hair out of her eyes. "We have journeyed far," she said, her eyes full of sorrow and her voice trailing off in the wind. "We have brought my son's grandfather to rest with Manitou in the land of his birth. He has little breath left and needs no doctor. He lives only to see his resting place."

"Perhaps someone in the general store or the tavern will know this place you speak about," Mother insisted. "We will take you there. Come."

Mother hugged Caroline close against her as they headed back down the road. The strangers and their horse followed behind. "This shouldn't take but a few minutes, Caroline. Are you warm enough?"

"Yes, ma'am," Caroline answered. The insides of her shoes were now filled with snow, and her socks, cold and damp from her toes to her ankles, had little pieces of ice dangling from the wool. Her neck itched beneath her scratchy woolen scarf, and she could feel the sting of the bitter wind through her coat and dress. But Caroline didn't mind. All she could think about was helping to find the place where boulders and fir trees stood watch by a creek.

"I don't think we should take them into the tavern or the general store, Mother," Joseph said, quietly enough so the wind wouldn't carry his words to the people trailing behind.

"Nonsense, Joseph," Mother said. "Why-ever not?"

"When I walked into the store, I heard Mr. Porter and two other men complaining about the Indians who keep coming back and roam-ing through the countryside, helping themselves to folks' crops and running off with their live-stock."

"Indians!" Caroline cried, her heart pounding. The last Indian she had seen had come into their frame house, taken their peacock feathers, and frightened them so badly that Caroline could still vividly remember his painted face and angry black eyes.

"Shush, Caroline," Mother scolded. "These people have done no such thing, Joseph. They've come to bury the boy's grandfather, and were your father here this minute, he would be searching up and down every creek this side of Milwaukee until he found those boulders and fir trees. He would have seen to it that the old man looked on his birthplace one last time before he died. I intend to do no less!"

"But what about the Indian who came to our house? He took our peacock feathers and left with a crock of our preserves!" Joseph said.

"That man was trying to find the white man who killed his brother. Mr. Carpenter told us as much," Mother said. "Besides, he did us no harm."

"But he came into our house, Mother," Caroline said. "He took our things . . ."

"There are good and bad men of all kinds, Caroline," Mother said sharply. "If it weren't for Father's Indian friends bringing us meat last winter, who knows where we might have found food to eat. The woman and her boy need our help, same as we have needed other folks' help. 'Freely ye have received, freely give.' So shall it be."

Mother marched across the snowy road and stopped outside Bebber's Tavern. A soft yellow glow filled the two crooked windows beside the wooden door. "I'll ask here, first, since it's the first place we've come to," she decided.

Caroline waited while Mother told the woman and boy her plan. Mother then took Caroline's hand and led her and Joseph into the tavern. Caroline had never been inside a tavern, and didn't know what to expect. Years ago, on her trips to town with Father, she had often passed the tavern and heard music and singing and bursts of laughter tumbling from the open windows. Caroline thought the tavern must be a wonderful place to visit, but Father said it was a place where men took care of business, and women, minding their business, left men alone. Even though she sometimes saw ladies going in and out of the noisy building after that, Caroline didn't wish she could visit the tavern anymore. And no matter how much she wanted to help the old man find his resting place, she wished Mother had decided to go to the general store to ask for directions first.

The small room was hot and smoky. A tall bench ran along the back wall, stacked with bottles, glasses, and mugs. Empty tables and chairs filled the room, and a small wooden piano sat close to the windows. Many of the brown piano keys were chipped or cracked, and a few were missing. Beside the piano, a fair-haired man sat leaning backward on his chair's rickety legs. Nearby sat another man who was hunched over a table, resting his bearded chin on a pewter mug.

"Don't speak a word, children," Mother ordered, "and stay behind me."

"Is that you, Mrs. Quiner?" a man's exuberant voice called out from the far side of the room. "Darned if it isn't! What in Sam Hill brings you here?" The voice came closer and closer, and a man with rosy cheeks and dark-brown hair combed loosely in an arc over his head was suddenly standing in front of Mother. His green flannel shirt was unbuttoned at the neck and his thumbs were tucked beneath his gray suspenders. The man held a cigar between his teeth, and when he smiled his bright smile, the cigar slid to one corner of his mouth.

"I'm hopeful that you can give me directions, Mr. Bebber," Mother answered.

"I can surely try, ma'am," the tavern owner answered, pulling the cigar out of his mouth. "Good day to you, children."

Caroline didn't know if she should answer, since Mother had clearly told her not to speak, but she decided to be polite instead of obedient. "Afternoon, sir," she said.

"Good day, sir," Joseph echoed.

"We're looking for a place where a row of boulders and firs stands watch by running water," Mother continued. "I have reason to believe it's someplace along one of the creeks in town. Can you think of any such place?"

"Sounds like Injun talk to me, Will!" the man leaning back on his chair bellowed. "Don't you be giving directions to no varmints!"

"A caution to you, Johnson," Mr. Bebber retorted. "Shut pan, 'fore I ask you to leave." A lock of hair fell across his forehead as he turned back to Mother and shook his head apologetically. "Could be a number of places, ma'am," he said. "I'm afraid I can't pin it down for you with so little to go on."

"Thank you," Mother said, turning toward the door and ushering Caroline and Joseph back into the shrill wind. "We'll go to the general store now, children," she said. "Mr. Porter or someone in town must know where to find such a place. If only Mr. Carpenter were here, he'd surely know the answer. He knows this land better than anybody."

"I could go for him, Mother," Joseph offered.

"In this storm?" Mother's voice was unsure.

"If I go full chisel, we could be back in no time," Joseph said.

"Then go, Joseph, but if the wind is too much for you, head straight home. Caroline and I will stop at every building along this side of road, and if we haven't any luck, we'll head down the other side."

Tugging on Mother's skirt as it billowed out in front of her, Caroline cried, "We could go to Anna's! Her father might know where to take the old man!"

"That's a fine idea, Caroline," Mother agreed, blinking away the wet snowflakes that were sticking to her eyelashes. "We will wait at Anna's until you return, Joseph."

"Yes, ma'am," Joseph said, and ran off down the snowy road toward home.

Mother hurried over to the woman and boy huddled together in the middle of the road, and Caroline followed. "We've had no luck yet," Mother told them, "but we will keep trying. Shall I find a place for you to go rest and warm yourselves awhile?"

"We have only one place we must find," the woman said.

Mother nodded. Continuing down the road,

she and Caroline visited the general store, the blacksmith's, and the shoemaker's. The woman and her son waited patiently outside each building, their eyes becoming more and more discouraged as the wind whipped up and Mother closed every door behind her without bringing good news.

As the shoemaker waved good-bye for the second time that afternoon and Mother and Caroline plodded through a sloping snowdrift in front of the wheelwright's shop, Mother said, "If Anna's father doesn't know where the boulders are, then we will have to send these people on their way, Caroline. I fear there's little else we can do for them."

Caroline didn't say a word. She was numb with cold and longed to be back in her frame house, but she wanted the old man to find his resting place even more.

"And now it is *you* be out in a terrible storm!" Mr. Short exclaimed as he pulled open the door and found Mother and Caroline standing there. "Come in, come in, Mrs. Quiner!" he said, stepping back and welcoming them into the shop. "Has anything happened?"

"Mother!" Joseph's voice rang out behind them. "I've brought Mr. Ben!"

Caroline whirled around to see her neighbor and brother jumping off Mr. Carpenter's sled. "Where are they, Charlotte?" Mr. Carpenter called out.

"We just left them in Mr. Hulsey's stable," Mother answered quickly.

"Left who?" Mr. Short asked, his curls blowing about as he stepped outside and shut the door behind him.

"Some travelers have come to town, searching for a place where a row of boulders and fir trees stands watch by running water," Mother explained. "They've traveled far with an old man who has little time to live and wants to see this place one last time."

"It must be along the creek that cuts right here through town and heads south through my land," Mr. Carpenter said as he walked up to the storefront. "The creek over your side doesn't have any fir trees to speak of. I'll help them from here, Charlotte. I've brought along the sled and the oxen, and I can quick search up and down the creek faster than any of us could on foot." Turning to Joseph, he added, "You get your mother and sister home, son. Safe, and quick as possible."

"Joseph can go along with you, Benjamin, and look for the boulders while you lead the team," Mother insisted.

"I'll go along for the ride if you don't mind, friend," Mr. Short broke in. He was standing in the bitter wind, hugging himself and bouncing up and down on his toes. "Then Joseph can see the ladies home."

"Thank you kindly." Mother gratefully relented. "My children are at home waiting for supper, and I'm afraid I've kept Caroline and Joseph out far too long already."

"Of course, ma'am," Mr. Short said. "Just one minute while I get my coat and tell my Anna I'll be going."

"Will she be all right by herself?" Mother asked with concern.

"Anna?" Mr. Short grinned. "She'll have the whole magazine Caroline kindly lent her read clear through by the time I return!"

"Please, Mother," Caroline asked. "Could I just say hello?"

"I don't see why not, Caroline." Mother's green eyes smiled for the first time all afternoon. "Run along inside while I tell the woman and her boy that Mr. Carpenter and Mr. Short are going to help them."

Caroline visited with Anna until Mr. Short was all bundled up and ready to go. Waving good-bye to her friend, Caroline crossed the road and waited while Mr. Short and Mr. Carpenter climbed into the sled, jerked the reins on the oxen, and led the woman, her son, and the horse down the final path of their long journey. The travois and the old man trailed along slowly behind, bumping up and down on the snow-covered road.

"May the good Lord watch over you," Mother said with a final wave. "Come now, children," she said when everyone was out of sight. "We must be on our way."

The wind's rancor prevented all conversation as Caroline, Joseph, and Mother crunched down the road as quickly as they could. Caroline's frozen, wet feet and toes smarted with every step, and suddenly she felt more tired than cold. She tried with all her might to think about warming up in front of the merry fire that would be waiting in the hearth, eating supper, and telling Martha, Henry, and Eliza about their exciting afternoon. But try as she might, she couldn't stop thinking about the face of the old man as he stared up at the sky.

"Do you think they will find his resting place, Mother?" Caroline asked hopefully.

"I am certain of it," Mother said, sliding her arm beneath Caroline's. "By nightfall the old man will be home."

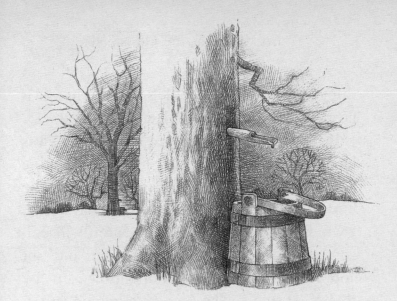

Maple Frolic

"Mr. Ben says the days are just now getting warm enough and the nights staying chilly enough for the sap to start running, Mother. He asked if we'd come help him and Charlie for the next few weeks," Henry announced, dropping his last armful of logs into the wood box and clapping the stray splinters and dirt off his hands. "He said we had to ask you first, seeing how it means we'll have to miss some days of school."

Holding a needle up to the firelight, Mother shut one eye and poked a strand of black thread through the needle's tip. "What is it he needs help with exactly?" she asked.

Joseph looked up from where he was kneeling in front of the hearth, scooping ashes into a small tin to sprinkle over the burning embers that remained at day's end. "Mr. Ben . . . um, Mr. Carpenter," Joseph corrected himself, knowing Mother did not approve of her children calling grown-ups by their first name, "he says he's hoping to tap twice the usual number of trees this spring so he can have enough maple sugar to last the year, and some to spare. Tomorrow or the day after, he and Charlie are planning to hammer the cedar spiles into the maple trees. They made all sorts of extra buckets to put under the spiles and catch the running sap. Henry and I won't help until the buckets are full. We'll collect the sap and bring it back to the kettles that are all set up for boiling. We'll also help chop wood so Mr. Ben, I mean Mr. Carpenter, can keep the fires burning beneath all three kettles."

"You may just as well call him Mr. Ben, Joseph, as the rest of your sisters and brothers do," Mother responded. "Try as I may, I can't insist on you calling the man Mr. Carpenter if even he calls himself Mr. Ben. The manners out here in this wilderness!" She shook her head.

"Mr. Ben says we can take turns stirring the hot sap too," Henry said excitedly. "Father never let us do that."

"It's been three years since we've tapped our own maple trees!" Mother sighed. "I recollect that you were just eight years old then, Henry-O, and not all that much taller than the kettles hanging over the open fires. It's a difficult job, stirring the heavy syrup without burning it or burning yourself. Father was right to keep you away."

Pushing his hair out of his eyes, Henry bragged, "I chopped wood for Father without ever once missing a log! I carried all the heavy buckets from under the trees over to the hot kettles and tipped them in without spilling a drop of the sap or making it splash out of the kettle! If I was old enough to do all that, then I was likely old enough to stir the syrup!"

"Must we listen to him and his stories?" Martha asked, tossing her brother a look of disdain.

"Certainly not to that kind of proud talk," Mother said reprovingly. "That's quite enough, Henry-O."

"Yes, ma'am," Henry said, winking over at Caroline.

"Mr. Ben says that if we can help, Mother, he'll gladly give us half of the first sap he collects," Joseph said peaceably. "So we'll get the best sugar, same as him. We can take some of the later sap home to make molasses too," he added. "But Mr. Ben thought my telling you about the first sap would convince you to let us help him."

"And he's right." Mother smiled. "There's nothing I'd like more than some fresh maple sugar! You may help Mr. Ben for as long as he needs you, boys. But I expect you to spend your evenings learning the lessons you're

missing in school instead of playing checkers. Spring's here, and your schooling's almost finished until after the harvest."

"Yes, ma'am," Joseph replied dutifully as Henry slapped his knee and shouted, "Yeehaw!"

"Oh please, Mother, couldn't I help too?" Martha dropped her knitting on her lap and clasped her hands together. "I'm a whole year older than Henry was when he helped Father tap the trees and make maple sugar!"

"Martha, you know that I need your help in the house more than ever since Grandma's left," Mother said. "Joseph and Henry will be plenty of extra help for Mr. Carpenter."

Dragging heavy buckets across the forest and stirring kettles full of boiling sap over a blazing fire did not sound at all like something Caroline wanted to do. It sounded almost as tiring as hauling water from the creek and wringing out wet clothes on washday, except it had to be done in the snow and cold instead of the warm sunshine, which made it even worse. Caroline didn't remember making maple syrup with Father years ago, but she did remember pulling sticky pieces of candy out of the snow and chewing every sweet, delicious bite. She also remembered Henry bounding through banks of snow, trying to sneak a piece of the taffy before anybody else discovered Mother making it. "Maybe we could just go help Mr. Ben at the very end of the day, Mother," Caroline suggested, "when all that syrup is stuck to the bottom of the pan! Remember how you spooned it out for us and swirled it over the snow till it got hard as can be and turned into stringy taffy? That's the part I want to help with, please!"

"I could help with that too," Eliza offered readily.

"Thomas string taffy too!" Thomas exclaimed. Standing in front of the wall opposite the hearth, he was twisting his fingers and hands into different shapes, casting shadows on the wooden beams of the wall with the help of the glowing firelight.

"If the boys help Mr. Carpenter and bring home some fresh maple sugar, the rest of us will be far too busy to go off sugaring," Mother said, very seriously.

"Busy?" Caroline asked, pulling a blue silk thread through the corner of the ivory linen she was cross-stitching.

"Getting ready for our very first Maple Frolic, of course!" Mother said, her green eyes sparkling merrily.

"A Maple Frolic?" the girls asked simultaneously.

"Henrietta Stoddard is hosting one this year. She's kindly invited us, and I'd like more than anything to visit her home. I've heard talk it's the grandest house in town," Mother said excitedly. "Mrs. Stoddard's told me she's planning to wear the dress I made her for Christmas. There will be music, and dancing, and all the guests will bring their own maple-sugar desserts. And knowing Mrs. Stoddard, we can expect a magnificent feast."

Caroline slumped in her chair, remembering the elegant dresses that Mother had often made for their neighbor Mrs. Stoddard. Spreading out the folds of her gray skirt, she examined it closely. In a few especially ragged places, the wool was almost worn through. Her dress had no lively print or color or interesting trim. Even Mother couldn't make this dress look pretty, Caroline decided, and Mother made the prettiest dresses that she had ever seen. "It's still too cold to wear our church dresses to the party, Mother, seeing how they have short sleeves," Caroline said sadly. "If Mrs. Stoddard's wearing one of her best dresses, how can we go to the very same party in our old everyday clothes?"

"We'll have perfectly fine dresses to wear, Caroline," Mother assured her. "Not long ago we received some lovely material."

"In the Christmas trunk!" Martha exclaimed.

"Indeed!" Mother laughed. "I was planning to surprise you with new dresses and trousers as soon as we can travel to church again this spring. I've already cut the material for each dress, and the boys' trousers won't take much more work. If I measure and pin all of you first thing tomorrow, I just may be able to finish your party clothes in time for the celebration. The frolic is two weeks away, after all. I'll be so busy sewing, it'll be as if I owned my dress shop again!"

"But what about you, Mother?" Caroline wondered. "What will you wear?"

"I can spruce up one of my old dresses with some fancy trim and new buttons, and wear it just fine." Mother smiled. "And if we're lucky enough to get another few days of winter cold or a mild snowfall during sugaring time, the sap will flow a bit longer, and I may just be able to make a dress for myself, too."

Martha jumped up from her chair. "We're going to a party!" she shouted.

"And we'll have new dresses!" Eliza gleefully clasped Martha's hands, and they spun around the room in circles.

"And buckets full of my favorite! Sugar syrup!" Caroline laughed, jumping up and down and joining the circle.

Setting her threaded needle and mending down neatly on the sewing table, Mother stood up, smoothed her skirt, and extended her arms in a grand gesture. "You'll have to learn to do more than twirl and hop if you're to dance at such a fine party, children," she teased, gathering the sides of her skirt and swishing it from side to side. "I'll have to teach you every jig I can remember!"

Mother and the boys quickly carried the chairs away from the center of the room and slid the table out of the way. After arranging the children in a line from tallest to shortest, Mother jigged to her place in front of them, slowly calling out steps as she danced them. The fire in the hearth squeaked and popped and danced along as the girls swayed, the boys bowed, Thomas ran in circles around the room, and Mother clapped and counted each step.

Watching Mother's graceful movements intently, Caroline tried to imitate her every step and gesture. But now and again her feet hopped where she didn't want them to go, and sometimes they got all mixed up with each other. Even worse, each time she tried to switch partners with Martha or Eliza, she bumped into Henry, Joseph, or Mother and burst into a fit of giggles before linking arms with the right partner and spinning around as she was supposed to.

Shifting black shadows rolled along the walls as Mother and the children danced around the room. Henry stamped and clapped louder than everyone else, crashing into the table and chairs on more than one occasion and shouting, "Swing your partners! Swing your partners!"

Mother curtsied one last time and fell breathless into her rocker, laughing with delight. "Enough!" she gasped. "You'll be a fine group of dancers, I think! But for now, off to bed with you!"

Still swirling and curtsying in her mind, Caroline finished tying the strings of her nightcap and climbed under the covers with Eliza and Martha. Closing her eyes, she softly tapped her toes up and down beneath the quilt, Mother's counting still ringing in her ears. Martha drummed her fingers on the pillow, while Eliza hummed softly and wiggled her foot from side to side. It took many of Mother's sweet, soft lullabies floating up to the rafters from her rocker below to finally quiet the room and send Caroline and her sisters off to sleep.

Each morning for the next two weeks, Henry and Joseph left the house before daylight to help Mr. Carpenter and Charlie collect sap and make maple sugar. Mother worked tirelessly, measuring, stitching, cutting, and trimming the girls' dresses. Though she couldn't wait for the Maple Frolic, Caroline wished for just one more snowfall so Mother would be able to finish the girls' dresses and still have time to make a new dress for herself.

Two days before Mrs. Stoddard's party, Caroline awakened to discover that her wish had come true. The white light brightening the room was different than the usual golden glow of morning sunlight. Caroline stretched as high as she could to look out the window on the far side of the room, but the frost-covered panes weren't letting any sunlight sneak through. Sighing happily, Caroline fell back to her pillow and pulled the quilt up under her chin, trying to imagine the beautiful party dress that Mother would now be able to make for herself.

"I suspect the frolic will be delayed a week or so," Mother called out from the stairs. Her straight black hair was not yet braided, and fell softly around her shoulders. "The sap in the trees will surely run for at least another week after this cold snap, and we should have just enough time to finish all our dresses, *and* make a very special maple sweet to bring to the party! Wake up everyone, Caroline." She smiled. "We have plenty of work and tasting to do!"

Bounding out of bed, Caroline did as she was told and then dashed across the drafty wooden floorboards to pull her clothes out of the chest. She had so much to look forward to: a new party dress, maple-sugar sweets, dancing, and a grand house to visit. One whole week of days could not pass quickly enough.

Mrs. Stoddard's House

"It's just about ready," Mother said, dipping her wooden spoon into the dark sap bubbling gently on the stove. She slowly lifted a spoonful above the rim and tipped the spoon over. A smooth, shimmering stream of creamy liquid flowed back into the pot. "No doubt about it," she decided, moving the iron pot away from the heat, "I've let it boil down as thick as I dare."

Turning to the children, who were hovering around the stove waiting patiently for a taste, Mother said, "It's time to make our maple sweet for the frolic! Boys, fill four buckets with the freshest, cleanest snow you can find and bring them inside, quick as a wink. Martha, spoon some flour into a cup, please, and bring it over to the table. Be careful not to spill any."

"What can I do, Mother?" Caroline asked.

"You may come along with me to the cellar, Caroline, and pick out some sprigs of mint while I get the butter."

"Mint?" Caroline asked. "What for?"

"To flavor the syrup," Mother answered. "Eliza, please tuck Thomas into the trundle for a quick nap. It will be time to get dressed for the frolic as soon as we finish making the sweets, and I'd like him to get some rest before then."

Mother pulled the heavy door up from the floor and climbed down into the dark cellar, with Caroline following close behind. The light from Mother's lantern flickered about the stone walls in the cool, fragrant room, and Caroline squinted as she stepped onto the dirt floor.

"The mint is over there with the other herbs," Mother said, pointing to the farthest corner of the cellar, where a few remaining bunches of dried herbs tied with fuzzy strands of twine hung upside down from the ceiling. "You need only pull one sprig, Caroline. I just want to give the syrup a touch of the flavor."

"Yes, ma'am," Caroline replied. Being careful not to bump into anything, Caroline wound her way past three barrels and a shelf full of crocks where vegetables, meat, and jam had been stored this past fall and winter. Most of the crocks and barrels were now empty. She stepped cautiously around a wide crate that contained the last four eggs from fall. Coated with fat to keep them fresh, they lay safely tucked in a nest of sawdust.

Standing beneath the hanging herbs, Caroline looked up at the leafy bundles, wondering which one was the mint that Mother wanted. The leaves on every hanging plant were a grayish-green color, and most of them were different shapes and sizes. Each tiny leaf had crinkled and curled into itself, and none of them looked like they belonged in a maple sweet.

"Is this one mint, Mother?" Caroline finally asked, pointing above her head.

Mother squinted across the cellar. "That's basil," she answered. "The mint is behind it. Next to the sage and the tarragon."

Caroline had heard of sage and tarragon and basil, but she certainly didn't know how to tell them apart. Moving beneath another hanging plant, she examined its thick spine and leaves. "This?" she asked.

"No, that's sorrel," Mother told her. "Count three more plants, Caroline: sweet woodruff, linum, sage. There! You're standing beneath the mint now. Smell it and see."

Reaching up, Caroline gently tugged a thin stalk until it came lose from the knotted twine. A scattering of dried leaves broke off the stem and fluttered to the ground. Caroline held the herb to her nose. "It smells sweet, Mother," she said in between sniffs. "It must be the mint."

"Good," Mother replied. "I've got the brick of butter. Let's get back upstairs."

Pushing aside a curvy strand of hanging onions, Caroline climbed upstairs into the bright room. Two buckets of snow were waiting beside the door, and Joseph and Henry had already hurried back outside to get another two. Eliza sat waiting by the table, swinging her legs impatiently beneath her seat. Martha waited there as well, holding a tin cup of flour.

"We've got all the ingredients ready," Mother determined as she placed the butter on the table and turned toward the stove. "Now all we need is some maple syrup."

Mother scooped a dipperful of the thick syrup out of the pot with her iron ladle and poured it into a wide bowl. Caroline, Martha, and Eliza watched as Mother dropped a chunk of butter on top of the steaming brown syrup and it melted into a creamy white puddle. Mother whipped the syrup and butter with a wooden spoon until it was blended, sprinkled a handful of flour over the top, and stirred the mixture again. Finally she said, "Now each of you take a mint leaf and crumble it into the bowl."

Caroline pulled a shriveled leaf from the dried stem and passed the sprig along to Martha and Eliza. Peering into the bowl, she rubbed the leaf between her fingers and scattered the gray-green crumbs onto the syrup. After Martha and Eliza had tossed their mint into the bowl, Mother gave the mixture one final whipping and said, "It's ready to be chilled."

As Mother carried the buckets of snow to the table, Joseph and Henry came running back into the house with one more bucket, partially filled with snow and ice. "The sun's awful warm today, Mother, and the snow's mostly melted. This is all we could find."

"Thank you, Joseph, it should be plenty," Mother said. "Set it right here next to the other two, please."

Caroline, Martha, Eliza, Henry, and Joseph knelt beside the buckets and watched Mother drizzle thick bands of the syrupy mixture across the snow. She waited a few moments for the bands to chill and harden, then cut them into tiny squares and placed them on a flat tin.

"Oh please, may we have a taste now?" Eliza pleaded.

"You may each have one sweet square," Mother said, relenting. "But we'll save the rest for the party."

"Is that what you call them, Mother?" Caroline asked. "Sweet squares?"

"It's as good a name as any," Mother decided.

"No more questions!" Henry interrupted. "I want one of the whatever-it's-called right now!"

"Please," Mother reminded him.

"No more questions, please," Henry corrected himself slyly. Reaching for a square, he popped it into his mouth. "De-licious!" he shouted, his mouth still full.

Caroline chose a square from the tin and bit into the soft, chewy candy. It was still cold and dewy on the bottom, and had a fresh, tangy taste that reminded Caroline of a red-and-white-striped candy stick. She hadn't thought there could be anything she liked better than sugar syrup poured over hotcakes, but suddenly she had a new favorite treat.

"It's time to dress for the party," Mother said. "Wash up, girls, and hurry upstairs to dress. Your clothes are laid out on your beds. I'll brush and braid your hair after you are dressed, so sit and wait for me like good young ladies if you happen to finish dressing before I do." Turning to Henry and Joseph, she added, "Please wake Thomas and help him into his clothes, and then get dressed yourselves."

One step in front of her sisters, Caroline raced to the top of the stairs and looked over at the bed. Clasping her hands together joyfully, she gushed, "Martha, Eliza, look! Our dresses!"

The girls' new dresses lay on top of the quilt beside a pile of white cotton stockings and petticoats. All three were made from the red fabric that had arrived in the Christmas trunk. The red cotton was woven in plaids, and Mother had trimmed each collar, sleeve, and hem with a delicate white lace that was detailed with diamonds and dots. Tiny white buttons fell in a perfectly straight line from the middle of the collar down to the bright red sash that hugged each waistline, and the skirts were full and flouncy. Caroline was certain that Mother had never made them prettier dresses.

The girls chatted and giggled as they pulled on their stockings and petticoats and helped each other into their new dresses. When all their buttons were buttoned and all their shoes were laced, they walked slowly down the stairs and waited for Mother. For a few moments Caroline sat quietly, just as she knew a young lady was supposed to wait, but then she just couldn't help standing up and spinning around in front of the hearth, watching the folds of her lovely dress fan out in a whirling blur of red plaid.

"Caroline!" Mother's voice called out from across the room. "We aren't at the party yet!"

Caroline felt her dress fall down around her legs as she stopped instantly, and turned to face Mother. "I'm sorry," she began. "Oh, Mother!" she breathed. "You are so pretty!"

Mother was standing on the far side of the

hearth, where the soft glow of firelight made her gold-colored dress shine richly. She had styled her hair so that it curved down below her ears and gathered in a bun at the nape of her neck. Little black ringlets framed her face and fell softly about her shoulders. The curved neckline of Mother's dress fell just below the ringlets, and the shoulders of her sleeves puffed into perfect circles. Tightly gathered at the elbows, the sleeves then hugged her arms down to her wrists. The dress's simple bodice fit snugly to her waist, where the flowing, lustrous silk brocade suddenly flared out into a golden bell skirt. As Mother glided across the room to help the girls brush and braid their hair, Caroline thought she looked just like an angel.

"You are so pretty, Mother," Eliza echoed.

"Not nearly as pretty as my girls!" Mother looked at her daughters proudly. "Your dresses fit just fine."

"Our dresses are so perfect, Mother," Martha crowed, "there won't be any other girls at the party who will look nearly as fine!"

" 'Let another man praise thee, and not thine own mouth, Martha,' " Mother cautioned. "Come now, we must hurry. The frolic won't wait for us!"

As Martha braided Eliza's hair, Mother brushed Caroline's until it shone, braided it, and tied the braid with a red gingham bow. "I had some material left over when I finished your dresses," she told the girls. "I thought you might like ribbons to match."

"Thank you, Mother." Caroline beamed, pulling her long brown braid over her shoulder to see her new ribbon. Henry bounded down the stairs that very moment with Joseph and Thomas close behind. The boys were wearing new navy-blue trousers, clean, starched white shirts, and suspenders. They had even neatly parted and combed their hair.

"Put on your coats and shawls, children, and we'll be on our way," Mother said as she began to bundle up Thomas. "Mrs. Stoddard may live just down the road, but we should dress for the cold weather, all the same."

Caroline hated to cover her new dress with

her old woolen shawl, but she didn't want to miss one single moment of the party, so she didn't complain. Wrapping the shawl around her shoulders, she followed her family out into the chilly March air.

The sun was playing hide-and-seek with the clouds, tossing columns of sunlight and shadows back and forth across the land. The cold spring breeze coursed through the leafless trees, and fallen leaves hopped along the wet brown earth. Caroline searched the trees and ground for the barest hint of green, but she didn't see any. She listened for a bird's cheerful song announcing that spring was finally here, but she didn't hear a single chirp. The merry chatter of townsfolk strolling down the road to Mrs. Stoddard's house filled the air, though, and their blue, red, green, and yellow hats, coats, mittens, and skirts brightened the drab brown of the landscape.

"We're here, children," Mother soon said. "Remember to mind your manners and greet Mrs. Stoddard respectfully, please."

Caroline looked up at Mrs. Stoddard's house.

She had often passed the magnificent home on her way to the woods to collect acorns and beechnuts for Hog, and wondered what it looked like inside. Surrounded by maples and pines, the house was set back majestically from the road. Two tall stories high with chimneys at either end and a shingled roof that angled upward to a steep point, the house was much larger than any other in town. Slender glass windows adorned all four sides, and Caroline could hardly keep herself from peeking through the front window that was set beside the great oak door.

Once inside the house, Caroline could hardly believe her eyes. The parlor to her left was crowded with gentlemen wearing fine vests and boots, and ladies dressed in their most elegant outfits. Young children ran about, trying their best to avoid bumping into the large settee and rosewood chairs neatly arranged in the center of the room. A stenciled pattern of wine-colored roses decorated the walls, and rich, velvety drapes framed every tall window and doorway. The mantel above the blazing hearth was filled with treasures: a wooden clock with gold hands, a china dove, and a pair of silver candlesticks. A large black-and-white picture of a man with shiny black hair and a fancy mustache watched the guests from a heavy gold frame in the center of the mantel. In a far corner of the room, a large piano gleamed, its ivory and ebony keys waiting to be played. And above all the cheerful chatter floated the joyful strains of a fiddle. Caroline had never imagined a scene so lovely.

"Mrs. Quiner! I am so happy to see you!" Mrs. Stoddard welcomed Mother with a sweet, clear voice, and Caroline nearly jumped in surprise.

"Good day, Mrs. Stoddard," Mother greeted her neighbor, and began to introduce her children one by one.

"Hello, dear," Mrs. Stoddard patted her hand when it was Caroline's turn to greet her hostess. "How lovely your dress is. I expect your mother made it for you?"

"Yes, ma'am," Caroline answered. "She

made hers, mine, and my sisters' too! And all the boys' clothes too!"

"She made my dress as well," Mrs. Stoddard confided. Her sparkly silver-white hair was neatly caught up in a bun, and she was wearing the rich black dress trimmed with ivory lace that Mother had finished making the week before Grandma left for Milwaukee. "I think it is almost as fine looking as yours."

"Yes, ma'am." Caroline nodded. "And almost as pretty as your house!"

"Thank you, Caroline." Mrs. Stoddard laughed. "Would you and your sisters like to come along and see the rest of it? We should bring your dessert into the dining room and place it with the rest of the treats."

"Oh yes, please!" Caroline, Martha, and Eliza said eagerly.

"But your guests . . ." Mother said.

"They'll entertain themselves until I return," Mrs. Stoddard assured Mother with a gentle pat on the shoulder. Turning her attention to Henry, Joseph, and Thomas, she added,

"Boys, I do believe you'll find some of your friends in the parlor. Feel free to join them if you're not interested in touring the house with your sisters."

"Yes, ma'am," the boys thanked their hostess, and disappeared.

Lifting her cane, Mrs. Stoddard walked slowly down a long hall and turned into a room that was as big as the parlor, and crowded with chairs, cabinets, and tables. Near the entrance to the room, two wooden dish dressers stood beside each other, grapevines and pears stenciled along their curvy tops and sides. Blue-and-white china bowls, plates, and serving dishes filled the shelves of the first dish dresser, and a matching pitcher and round platter stood proudly on the top shelf beside a glass vase that was filled with dried flowers.

"May I look at the dishes please, ma'am?" Caroline couldn't help asking.

"Why, of course, child," Mrs. Stoddard answered.

Moving closer to the dish dresser for a better look, Caroline marveled at the tall buildings and stately homes painted on each plate and bowl. "What places are these?" she asked politely.

"That is the statehouse in Boston," Mother answered, looking over Caroline's shoulder.

"And the rest of the engravings are of Boston estates," Mrs. Stoddard added. "I packed all this china and brought it from my home in Massachusetts. My husband wanted to leave it behind, but I insisted it make the journey with us. The china has been in my family for some thirty years."

"Come see! Over here!" Martha burst out. She was standing in front of the other dish dresser looking excitedly at the shelves.

Caroline hurried to Martha's side. On the bottom shelf of the cabinet, green, blue, red, yellow, and orange bottles in all shapes and sizes twinkled in the firelight. Above the bottles, Caroline discovered a row of delicate porcelain figures smiling painted smiles at her. Caroline had seen bottles like this before on the storekeeper's shelves, but she'd never before seen such figurines. Standing on her tiptoes, she stared at the miniature painted people, longing to hold one of the tiny figures in her hand.

"Aren't they the prettiest little people you ever saw?" Martha asked.

"I can't see so high up!" Eliza complained.

"My, but they are exquisite," Mother said, lifting Eliza up into her arms for a look.

"I've been collecting them since I was a child," Mrs. Stoddard told them. "Come now, let's put your treats on the table so the children can go dance and play."

Caroline continued to gaze longingly at the porcelain figures until Martha tugged on her sleeve. Reluctantly she followed her older sister past the enormous hearth. Stones as round and wide as pumpkins surrounded the hearth and climbed straight up to the ceiling. Mighty flames leaped high above Caroline's head, and the smell of the crackling logs mingled with all the other sweet and spicy smells in the air.

"I'll bet you'd never get cold in this house," Martha whispered to Caroline.

"Or hungry, either," Caroline whispered back as Mrs. Stoddard led them to the two long tables on the opposite side of the room that overflowed with delicacies: pork, duck, chicken, and venison; codfish and whitefish; baked beans and fruit stuffing; stewed squash and potatoes; pickled cucumbers; baked bread, fresh butter, and currant jam; dried blackberry and pumpkin pies; and tins piled high with cookies and maple treats. Mother put her sweet squares down at the edge of the table, and Caroline watched closely to see where she set the tin. No other sweet on the table would taste as good as Mother's, Caroline was certain, and she wanted to know just where to find them when she came back to the table for dessert.

"We'll be eating soon enough," Mrs. Stoddard promised as a great roar of laughter and applause burst from the parlor and the fiddler quickened his song. "The guests must have started dancing," she said. "Shall we join them, or would you like to see the sitting room first?"

231

"You should join the rest of your guests, Mrs. Stoddard," Mother decided.

"Oh please, Mother, may we see the sitting room for just one minute?" Martha asked.

"Please?" Caroline echoed, even though she knew she might get scolded for disagreeing with Mother. She hoped she would be able to visit Mrs. Stoddard's house again, but just in case she couldn't, she wanted to see every last corner of it.

"It won't take but a minute, Charlotte, and it seems everyone's having a fine time without me," Mrs. Stoddard said before Mother could answer. Leading her guests to the farthest end of the room, Mrs. Stoddard stepped through a low doorway and into a high-ceilinged study. A daybed was set against one wall, two high-backed chairs placed on either side. In the corner of the room, a mahogany rocker sat beside the large cast-iron box stove. Shelves stacked with books lined one wall from the floor to the ceiling. Framed drawings filled the opposite wall; horse-drawn carriages moving past tall buildings, ladies in long skirts and feather-tipped hats being escorted through crowded streets by gentlemen in black jackets and tall black hats, stately homes and gardens, were all brought to life by muted strokes of black ink.

"Goodness glory," Mother exclaimed as she studied the drawings, "did you sketch all of these, Mrs. Stoddard?"

"Over a period of many years, Charlotte," Mrs. Stoddard replied. "My late husband, James, insisted on framing and hanging each and every one of them. Rest his soul."

"Maybe he's the man with the curly mustache in that big picture above the fireplace," Caroline murmured quietly to Martha.

"They're splendid!" Mother said. "Look, girls, most of these sketches are scenes from Boston, where Grandmother and Grandfather Tucker live. They look just like the city I left before I married your father and journeyed west."

Caroline had heard of Boston many times before, but she had never seen pictures of it. Wandering slowly through the room, she admired the black-and-white scenes of spectacular houses set back on tree-lined lawns that stretched out grandly in front of them. To think that Mother and Mrs. Stoddard had once lived in such a place!

"I fear we ought to get back to our neighbors now," Mrs. Stoddard said. "But I'll be reading from *Robinson Crusoe* in this sitting room later this evening, girls. I do hope you'll come listen."

"Yes, ma'am!" Caroline and Martha exclaimed.

"Me too," Eliza chimed in.

The parlor buzzed with conversation and whirled with color as ladies and gentlemen danced and clapped merrily, and children twirled along. "Look, the boys are over by the piano with the Carpenters," Mother said, waving to them. "Let's go join them. I am eager to see Mrs. Carpenter."

"Charlie's there too!" Martha said excitedly, her cheeks blushing a bright pink. "Oh, I hope they haven't been waiting too long!"

"Come on over, Charlotte!" Mr. Carpenter bellowed from across the room. "I need three dancing partners, and only the most peart girls in red dresses and matching bows will do!"

The fiddle rejoiced as Caroline, Martha, and Eliza showed Mr. Carpenter the dance steps Mother had taught them. Henry, Charlie, and Joseph soon jigged onto the floor and Mr. Carpenter disappeared into the crowd, leaving the children spinning and swinging from partner to partner until the fiddle finished its song and the feast began.

"Save some room for dessert," Mother advised as Henry heaped food onto his plate and then added extra helpings onto Caroline's. "I'll eat whatever you don't, little Brownbraid," he promised as they sat down with the others. Caroline left only three forkfuls of stuffing and a bite of bread for Henry to finish but still had enough room for three of Mother's tiny sugar squares and a taste of every other dessert on the table besides.

As daylight faded outside the plush curtains and the littlest heads in the parlor nodded off on their parents' shoulders, Mrs. Stoddard called the remaining children into the sitting room. "If you all sit in front of me, children, you will be able to hear, I'm sure," she said, settling herself in the rocking chair.

Caroline smoothed the red folds of her dress beneath her legs and sat down between Eliza and Henry as Mrs. Stoddard opened a shiny black book on her lap and began, "This passage is from *The Life and Adventures of Robinson Crusoe*.

" 'One day, about noon, going towards my boat, I was exceedingly surprised with the print of a man's naked foot on the shore, which was very plain to be seen on the sand. . . .' "

"My kind of story!" Henry whispered as Mrs. Stoddard continued the riveting tale in her sweet, melodic voice. But Caroline found it hard to pay attention to the words. Her eyes were drawn again and again to the shelves of books, the sketches and paintings, the tall windows, the velvety drapes and grand wooden furniture.

When Mrs. Stoddard finished the chapter and opened the second volume of stories resting on her lap, Caroline perked up and listened carefully, sighing as her hostess finished the final words of the tale:

" 'They could see she was a real princess and no question about it, now that she had felt one pea all the way through twenty mattresses and twenty more feather beds. Nobody but a princess could be so delicate.' "

The story of the princess and the pea was in one of the books that had arrived in the Christmas trunk. Mother had often read the story before bedtime, and Caroline had memorized almost every word. Today was the very first time she had ever felt the way a princess must feel, dressed in a beautiful dress and living in a magical place. She longed to stay at Mrs. Stoddard's house for just a little while longer, but Mother soon appeared in the doorway with Thomas sound asleep in her arms. It was time to go home.

"Thank you for having us, ma'am." She smiled at Mrs. Stoddard and wrapped her shawl around her shoulders.

"I do hope you enjoyed yourself and that

you'll visit again soon, Caroline," Mrs. Stoddard said warmly.

"I hope so too," Caroline said.

Twinkling stars cheered the blue-black sky as hazy white moonlight glazed the earth. Caroline breathed in the cold night air, recalling every wonderful moment of Mrs. Stoddard's frolic. Someday, maybe, she'd have china plates, porcelain figurines, shelves filled with books, and drapes as rich as the finest dresses. Even if she never got to be a princess.

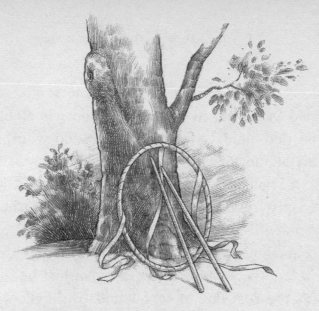

Game of Graces

Spring finally awakened the barren world. The cold, moist earth grew warm and dry. Silvery buds came out of hiding, blossoming into lush green leaves. Daisies, buttercups, violets, and clover turned the meadows into purple, yellow, white, and blue bouquets. Birds whistled, bees hummed, rabbits, squirrels, and field mice darted to and fro. Then spring disappeared as quickly as it had appeared, leaving the early days of summer in its stead.

Pausing at the top of a steep hill, Caroline

took a deep breath. "It looks the same," she said as she gazed at the one-room schoolhouse nestled amidst swaying grasses and wildflowers at the far end of the meadow.

"What did you expect?" Martha asked crisply, tossing her braids behind her shoulders with two quick jerks of her head. "A new schoolhouse?"

"You don't have to be so mean just because it's the first day of school and you don't want to go back!" Caroline snapped. Martha never liked school. And the first day of school she liked least of all.

"I wish I was a boy," Martha said. "Then I could be outside all summer and learn my lessons in the schoolhouse when it's cold and snowing and no one can go outside anyway!"

Caroline nodded, though she didn't agree. She wished she could go to school in the winter *and* in the summer. She couldn't wait to get back to the schoolhouse and begin her new lessons. Miss Morgan, the schoolmistress, would be there to greet her, and all the other students she hadn't seen through the long winter would be there too. "We'd best go now," she told Martha, suddenly in a hurry. "I want to be sure and get a good seat."

When they arrived, the school yard was empty. Caroline hurried into the schoolhouse, certain that everyone was already inside and sitting down. But the schoolhouse was as silent as the school yard had been. Only Anna was inside, and she had already chosen the best bench in the small room. Sunlight poured through the window beside her, brightening her mop of dark curls as she waited for Caroline and Martha to join her.

Caroline quickly slid into place beside her friend. "Have you seen Miss Morgan yet?" she asked. "She isn't ringing the school bell the way she did last summer."

"She isn't even here yet," Martha grumbled as she sat down beside Caroline. "See? Even the teacher wasn't in as big a hurry to get to school today as you were!"

"I wanted to get here early too," Anna said pleasantly. "The room's sure to get crowded, and I wanted to save us a good seat!"

"May I? Sit?" A soft voice interrupted haltingly.

Caroline turned at once toward the aisle. Elsa was standing there, looking through her long bangs and smiling shyly. "Of course, Elsa! We can move over some. Sit with us, please!"

"We're still waiting for Miss Morgan. She is not here yet." Martha spoke slowly to Elsa and slid so close to Caroline that their legs and arms touched. Elsa gratefully sat down beside Martha, raising the hem of her gray skirt up above her bare, dusty toes.

The benches soon filled with girls of all ages, scrubbed clean, braided, and dressed in calico and gingham. A few young boys squeezed together in one bench, ignoring the girls. All the students waited impatiently for the schoolmistress to appear. The chatter in the room was so loud that Caroline could hardly hear Anna and Elsa, and it grew louder and louder until the door to the schoolroom shut with a bang. Every head in the room turned to the door and watched, eyes wide open with surprise. A stranger was standing at the back of the room. He was almost as wide as he was tall, and as he walked to the front of the room, he had to turn sideways so he would fit into the narrow aisle that divided the room. When the man passed Caroline's row, she couldn't help staring in awe at his immense belly. Stuffed into a crisp white shirt and tucked beneath black suspenders, it stretched so far that Caroline was afraid the suspenders might snap.

Once he reached the front of the schoolroom, the man moved behind the wooden table and pulled out the chair beneath it. Caroline and Anna grabbed hands, waiting to see if the chair's spindly legs would support such a man. Holding on to the sides of the table, he slowly sat down. The chair groaned in protest.

"A good morning to you, students," he said in a deep voice. "My name is Mr. Speare. I am your new schoolmaster."

Caroline nearly shrieked "Ouch!" as Martha pinched her elbow hard. She looked at Martha, then at Anna and Elsa. The look of horror on their faces mirrored her own.

"Excuse me, sir," an older girl with freck-les bravely said. "What's happened to Miss Morgan?"

"She's married a fellow by name of Donald Jackson and moved on to Prairieville—er . . . Waukesha, I think they call it now," Mr. Speare corrected himself. "But she has left behind a journal full of notes, detailing your progress. Each of you shall continue your stud-ies wherever it is that you left off with her." Blotting his damp forehead with a white hand-kerchief that was stiff with starch, he droned on. "We will begin by entering your names in my roster. When you come to the front of the room one by one, I will also briefly discuss any notes Miss Morgan left pertaining to you. Do me the kindness of sitting quietly until you hear your name."

As Mr. Speare called the first student, Caroline shifted on the bench, her thoughts spinning. Why had Miss Morgan left without telling anyone? What kind of notes had she left for this new schoolmaster? And what sort of teacher would he be? Caroline studied the enormous man seated at the front of the room. His black hair was pasted down over his head, comb lines running through it. Stray black hairs sprang out in all directions from the furry eyebrows that nearly hid his small gray eyes. Unlike most men in town, he had no beard or mustache, only long sideburns that disappeared into his collar along with his cheeks and chins. Caroline searched the new school master's face, wondering if he would use the long wooden stick he had just placed beside a tall stack of books on the table.

The sun had climbed high in the sky and all its golden rays had disappeared from the room when Mr. Speare finally called Caroline's name. Trembling, she stepped over Martha and Elsa and walked the short distance to the front of the room.

"You are Caroline Quiner?" the schoolmaster inquired.

"Yes, sir," Caroline responded, trying to keep her voice steady.

"Miss Morgan writes that you have just begun your first reader and have completed more than half of the lessons in your spelling book," he said.

"Yes, sir," Caroline replied.

"Good for you, young lady." Mr. Speare sniffed, and blew his nose into his handkerchief with a loud *honk!* "Forgive me, child," he said, tucking his handkerchief into his sleeve. "As soon as you have finished every lesson in your spelling book, you should move on to the second speller. Do you know anyone who has the second speller, a sister or brother, perhaps?"

"Yes, sir," Caroline said. The speller Martha and both her brothers had used was faded and frayed at the corners, but Caroline didn't linger long enough to tell the schoolmaster about the book's tattered condition. The moment Mr. Speare finished saying, "Fine, Caroline. Please be certain to tell me before you begin using the new book," she dashed back to her seat.

"What's he like?" Martha whispered as Caroline sat down.

"He's not awful," Caroline replied honestly.

"He's not awful *yet*, you mean!" Martha declared. "Thank goodness it's almost time for dinner. He hasn't called my name yet, and I can wait till after recess or even till tomorrow to speak to him!"

As soon as Caroline sat down, Mr. Speare dismissed the students with a gentle reminder. "Return to your seats punctually, please, one hour from now." The last student had already fled out the door by the time the schoolmaster finally rose out of his seat.

"How could Miss Morgan just up and leave like that, without telling anybody?" Caroline was first to ask as she and Martha, Anna, and Elsa found a shaded grassy spot near some of their schoolmates and sat down to eat. Mother preferred that Caroline and Martha return home for dinner every day, but since today was the first day back to school, she had agreed to let them stay at the schoolhouse and eat dinner with their friends.

"I wish *I* could just up and leave," Martha grumbled, reaching into the tin pail she was holding. "I'd run as fast and as far from that schoolhouse as I could go!"

"I've got some bread, some cheese, and a cold piece of pork. Same as last night's supper," Anna announced. "What'd you bring?"

"Beans!" Elsa said proudly, as if she had been practicing the word all morning.

Martha pulled two crumbly yellow cakes out of the tin, handed one to Caroline, and tipped the tin upside down. "Nothing but cornmeal patties again," she complained. "I can hardly wait till the vegetables in the garden start growing and the wild berries get ripe. I'm tired of every meal being patty cakes or maple sugar poured over crumbs of bread!"

"You and Caroline can share some of my dinner," Anna offered. "Papa always sends me to school with too much."

"No thank you," Caroline answered as Anna laid out thick chunks of cheese and pork on a linen napkin. "Mother says it isn't polite to eat other folks' food," she added before

248

Martha could say anything.

"But I can't eat this much, and if you don't help me, it'll all go to waste," Anna countered. "And that's a far worse sin than eating other folks' food!"

"She's right, you know." Martha looked defiantly at Caroline as she accepted a piece of pork from Anna. "I'll happily keep you from being a sinner, Anna. Thank you!"

"Me too!" Caroline agreed, biting into the chunk of cheese that Anna handed her.

"Would you like some, Elsa?" Anna offered.

Elsa was sitting quietly across from Caroline and Martha, eating her beans and listening to every word. "No thank you," she finally said, dropping her spoon into her now-empty tin pail. "Play!"

"Play what?" Caroline asked.

Elsa pointed to two girls standing with their backs to them a few feet away. The girls were whirling a hoop decorated with bright ribbons back and forth to each other with two slim canes. "Play!" she repeated eagerly.

"They're playing the game of Graces, I think," Anna said. "Papa saw the wands and hoop in the general store a few months back. Mr. Porter told him the game's real popular, and Papa said he'd get a hoop from the cooper and make me a set of my own, if I want."

"Did you say yes?" Caroline asked. She couldn't take her eyes off the hoop soaring from girl to girl in a whirl of color. Its streaming colored ribbons fluttered through the air like a rainbow with wings.

"I told him he could make them for me soon as he finished all his other work," Anna explained. "But I don't think he'll ever finish all his other work."

"Henry or Joseph could whittle us some of those sticks and hoops in an evening or two, if we asked," Martha declared.

"And they could make extra wands so Anna and Elsa could play too," Caroline added excitedly. "Mother has a whole basketful of scraps from all the shirts and dresses she's made. I'm sure she'd give us one or two of the brightest-colored scraps to hang on the hoops instead of ribbons."

As the four girls intently watched the game of Graces, a crowd of their schoolmates gathered behind them. The ribboned hoop was flung from player to player, and twenty braided heads turned at exactly the same time to watch each toss.

"Oh, Martha," Caroline exclaimed, "maybe Henry and Joseph could make us the hoops and sticks tonight. Then we can bring them to school and play tomorrow!"

"Quiet, Caroline," Martha whispered into Caroline's ear. "It's those girls playing, the girls from church. The ones with the white gloves."

Caroline's smile disappeared as she looked from the spinning hoop to the players' faces. Martha was right. Caroline had been so enthralled by the colorful ribbons sailing through the air, she hadn't paid attention to the girls playing the game. They were dressed in matching blue-and-white print dresses that were trimmed with thick white ruffles. Their braids didn't hang down their backs or over their shoulders like those of all the girls watching their game. Instead, they hung from the sides of their heads in two braided circles and were tied with crinkly white ribbons right above each ear, where the bottom of the braids were pinned to the tops. Peeking out from beneath their ruffled hems were gleaming black shoes and white stockings, the very same shoes and stockings worn by the very same two girls who had snickered at Martha more than a year ago when she had gone to church in a new silk dress and hadn't worn any shoes. Caroline had defended her sister at the church and had stood by Martha in front of the schoolhouse weeks later as Martha had told the girls exactly what she thought of them. Ever since that day, Caroline had purposely ignored the awful pair in the schoolroom and in town whenever she happened to see them.

"Their dresses are even prettier than their hoop," Caroline sighed.

"Well, when we're finished with our hoops,

they will be even prettier than their dresses," Martha said determinedly.

"You should pay them no mind," Anna said sympathetically. "We have to go back inside now anyway."

Elsa and Martha followed the rest of the students into the schoolhouse, with Caroline and Anna a few steps behind. As they waited in line to file back into their bench, the two girls in the matching dresses stepped up beside Anna. Caroline stared straight ahead, pretending not to notice them and hoping that Martha wouldn't turn around and look for her any time soon.

"If you liked the hoop so much, you can see pictures of it in *The American Girl's Book*."

One of the girls was addressing Caroline, and she immediately recognized the voice. It was the same voice that had accused her sister of being a poor, wild country girl. "Or you can just get yourself one at the general store," the voice continued. "That's where we got ours. They come special made, all wrapped up in a package, and fly much better than the homemade kind."

"Thank you," Anna spoke up as Caroline stared silently ahead.

"They don't cost much, either," the second girl began.

"Much less than a pair of shoes," the first girl finished snidely.

"Shhh, Susannah! Mama says not to be mean to people just because they're poor and don't have lots of money like we do," the second girl said in a softer voice that was still loud enough for Caroline, and everyone else nearby, to hear.

"I'm not being mean, Esther," the first girl insisted. "I'd let them play with our hoop if they asked nicely and promised not to break it. Why, I'd even bring some extra food for them tomorrow and share it, just like Anna did today. They'd only have to ask us politely."

Caroline felt sick to her stomach. Her cheeks flushed red with shame and anger, and her fingers closed into tight fists at her sides.

"Don't let them bother you," Anna urged.

"I can't help it, Anna," Caroline answered through clenched teeth. "If she says one more word . . ."

"Even if they don't ask for any," the second girl continued, "I think we should just bring some extra food for them tomorrow. It would be the right and Christian thing to share what we have with those who are less fortunate."

The room fell silent as Martha whirled around and shouted, "What makes you so important that you can stick your nose into other folks' conversations? And what makes you think we'd ever want your food, or your silly hoop, or *anything* that belongs to the likes of you?" Her face was red with fury and her eyes were flashing as she pushed her way beside Caroline and stepped in front of Susannah. Glaring at her, Martha seethed, "If I wasn't standing here in a schoolroom full of girls who are nicer than you in every single way, I'd spit on your pretty dresses and smash your fancy hoop right over my knee till it broke into little tiny pieces, the perfect-size pieces for folks as small-minded as you!" Stamping her bare foot on the floor, Martha finished: "I told you once to keep your words to yourself, and I'm saying it again. Keep your awful words to yourself!"

"Who is it? Who is it spewing such venom in my schoolhouse!" Mr. Speare's angry voice demanded from the front of the room, where he stood on the tips of his scruffy boots, straining to see who was causing all the commotion. "Caroline Quiner! Is that you shouting like that? I demand that you not make such a fuss in my schoolhouse!"

Caroline looked from her sister's shocked face to Susannah's prim expression and thin, terrible smile. Turning to face the schoolmaster and all the students crowding the aisle in front of her, Caroline answered loudly, in the bravest voice she could muster, "Yes, I said it. I'm sorry, sir."

"She did not, Mr. Speare," Martha spoke up immediately. "I said every word. And I meant it, too."

"And who are you?" the schoolmaster questioned, his thick eyebrows raised in suspicion.

"Martha Quiner, sir," Martha answered.

"This is most peculiar," Mr. Speare said. "Two of you taking the blame for the atrocious conduct of only one. I'll ask you, again, Miss Caroline Quiner. Were you the cause of this scene?"

Caroline stared straight ahead at the schoolmaster, watching him drum his fingers on the table beside the long wooden stick. She didn't want to tell a lie, but she didn't want Martha to get in trouble, either. And she really *had* been the cause of all the trouble. She was the one who had most liked Susannah and Esther's hoop and had declared as much out loud, before she ever realized who was playing the game. She had also been the one standing beside the girls in line, in the perfect place for Susannah to humiliate her. She might not have shouted the words that caused the awful fuss in the classroom, but as she looked at Susannah's smug face once more, she wished with all her heart that she had uttered every single word. "Yes, sir," Caroline answered firmly. "It's all my fault."

"Caroline!" Martha gasped.

"Not another word, young ladies," Mr. Speare ordered. "It takes grit to tell such a truth in front of a whole schoolroom of people, so I shall not send you home. However," he continued, "I expect both you and your sister to remain in the schoolhouse after your lessons, Miss Quiner. You may not return home until every last inch of this schoolhouse is scrubbed clean."

"Yes, sir," Caroline said.

"All of you take your seats, now," Mr. Speare said loudly. "We've wasted more than enough time for one afternoon."

Caroline sat stiffly between Martha and Anna and stared down at her reader, waiting for the horrible afternoon to end. Blankly staring at the same page of meaningless letters and words, she never looked up until Mr. Speare dismissed the rest of the students for the afternoon.

"I said you may leave now," Mr. Speare repeated to a few lingering students as Caroline slowly got up from her bench.

"We'd like to stay and help. If we may, sir," Anna addressed the schoolmaster in a soft but determined manner.

"I stay also," Elsa said slowly.

"Most peculiar," Mr. Speare said, shaking his head in surprise. "Miss Morgan left word that there were troublemakers in this school-house, but none of your names was listed as such. Please close the door when you leave, young ladies. I shall see you in the morning."

Without speaking, the girls scrubbed the wooden benches, swept the wood-plank floors, and wiped Mr. Speare's slate board clean, before shutting the schoolhouse door behind them.

"My fingers stink like lye," Martha grimaced as she and Caroline waved good-bye to their friends and called out one final thank-you before heading off through the meadow.

"Mine, too," Caroline said.

"What you did today was braver than anything I ever saw," Martha said with admiration.

"No braver than your standing up to those awful girls." Caroline shrugged.

"Mr. Speare would have blamed me for the whole thing if he had called me up to the front of the room before recess and already knew my name," Martha mused. "I was just lucky that he knew yours instead of mine."

"It doesn't matter," Caroline answered honestly. "I just hope Mother doesn't get word of it."

"She won't from me," Martha promised.

"Me either," Caroline agreed.

"Maybe we can ask Henry and Joseph to start whittling away at a hoop and some sticks for us tonight," Martha said hopefully.

"No." Caroline paused. "I don't think that game is much fun after all."

"I guess I don't either," Martha said.

Mother didn't hear anything about the game of Graces or the trouble in school until weeks later. One evening Caroline and Martha told Henry, Henry told Joseph, and Joseph told Mother. After dinner the next day, Joseph traded for a hoop from the cooper, and later that night he and Henry sanded the hoop and whittled three perfect wands out of long, straight sticks. The very next morning Mother called the girls over to her sewing table the moment they had finished their chores. Lifting her basket full of scraps, she said, "Choose the brightest-colored ribbons and scraps of material you can find, girls. You'll have nothing less than the prettiest hoop in town by this afternoon, I daresay."

Corduroy Bridge

For the next few weeks Caroline worked especially hard at her lessons in the schoolroom and steered clear of Susannah and Esther in the school yard. One afternoon in late July she remained seated in the schoolhouse after Mr. Speare had dismissed the rest of the students.

"Excuse me, sir," she called from her bench.

"What is it, Miss Quiner?" The schoolmaster looked up from the pile of books he was stacking on the far side of his table.

"I've finished the lessons in my spelling

book, Mr. Speare," Caroline said, trying not to sound nervous. "You told me that I should come to you before I begin using the next speller."

"So I did." Mr. Speare nodded. "Did you bring along your copy?"

"Yes, sir," Caroline said, walking to the front of the room and handing the schoolmaster her slender gray book.

"Yes, this is the correct speller, Caroline," Mr. Speare commented as he quickly scanned the worn pages. "If you work just as hard to learn all these words, I've no doubt you'll be the finest speller in this school. Among students your age, of course."

"Thank you, sir." Caroline beamed. Tucking her new speller on top of her reader and book of sums in the crook of her arm, she rushed outside, where Martha was waiting.

"What'd Mr. Speare say?" Martha asked.

"That I should keep working hard at my lessons," Caroline answered without sharing the rest of the schoolmaster's praise. Martha sometimes had trouble with her spelling, and

Caroline didn't want to hurt her feelings.

"'Keep working hard at your lessons! Keep working hard at your lessons!'" Martha mimicked, scrunching up her nose. "Why does every old person always have to say 'Keep working hard at your lessons'?"

"I don't know," Caroline admitted. "Let's walk home by way of the creek," she added, changing the subject.

"Over the corduroy bridge?" Martha asked.

"Yes, let's!" Caroline exclaimed happily. On the edge of town the corduroy bridge cut across the marsh and the creek. It was made of a wide raft of logs that had been laid down carefully side by side. Caroline loved balancing on the logs, which shifted and rolled beneath her bare feet as she stepped from one to the next. "If we hurry, we'll get to cross over it two times and still make it home in time for supper!"

Caroline and Martha set off, the hot summer breeze blowing in their faces as they hurried along. Towering white clouds loomed over the fields and meadows, golden shafts of afternoon sunlight bursting through them and descending to earth like shimmering ladders connecting soil and sky. Knee-high grass and wildflowers bent this way and that, tickling Caroline's bare legs as she ran along. They neared the creek, and the meadow was soon edged by marshland. Wildflowers grew side by side with velvety brown cattails, and the scatterings of marsh milkweed tinted the wetlands a soft pink.

"We're almost there," Caroline said, running her fingers along the tips of spiky cattails springing up from the mud.

"I know," Martha answered. "What's that noise?"

Caroline stopped and listened. The still summer air was alive with the buzz of mosquitoes and flies. Muskrats rustled about as crickets chirruped, and the songs of redwinged blackbirds, perched about the cattails, lilted across the marsh. Beneath these sounds of summer, a tinny blast, followed by a thump and a rattle, grew louder and louder.

"I don't know what it is, but it's coming from the bridge, I think!" Caroline said.

"Let's go see!" Martha cried.

Braids flying, Caroline and Martha dashed to the corduroy bridge, clutching their school-books and running as fast as the thick maze of cattails would allow.

"It's music!" Caroline called out to Martha in between breaths. "A fife like Anna's, and a bugle . . . and a drum, I think!"

"Two drums, at least," Martha shouted back. "One boom's louder than the other."

As the rolling logs of the corduroy bridge came into view, the music stopped. In the distance Caroline could see a short line of people crossing the bridge in single file. Fifes and bugles bobbed up and down as the men extended their arms in an attempt to keep their balance. The whole group was dressed in dark-blue shirts and trousers. Plumed white feathers flounced out of the fiery red hats poised atop their heads, and sashes in the same bold color cut diagonally across their shirts from shoulder to hip.

"It's a parade!" Caroline shouted.

"It must be a whole band! Keep going,"

Martha urged. "I want to see it up close."

As Caroline and Martha reached one side of the bridge, the last member of the band was stepping off the opposite side of the bridge and heading toward town. "We missed it!" Martha called out in dismay, falling backward to the ground and dropping her armful of books.

A swirling cloud of tiny black flies circled frenetically around Caroline as she plunked down on the ground beside her sister, gasping for breath. "I couldn't go any faster," Caroline puffed. "I have an awful stitch in my side as it is!"

"Let's sit for a minute," Martha gasped. "Then we'll cross the bridge and go home."

Still catching her breath, Caroline began batting at the flies. "Pesky things!" she grumbled, wiping sweat from her forehead and slapping a tiny gnat that landed on the back of her neck.

A great clattering suddenly shook the air, followed by the piercing blast of a bugle. Caroline and Martha scrambled to their feet and watched as two sleek black horses and a wide wagon rumbled up to the edge of the bridge. The horses set their shoes on the first log of the bridge tentatively, only to whinny loudly and step back onto solid ground.

"Git on with ya!" a man shrieked. Stunned, Caroline looked over at the driver of the wagon, who was shouting at the horses, his face one big snarl. Pulling on the reins with one hand, he furiously shook a bugle over his head with the other. "It's a blasted bridge, dash it all! And we've seven more miles to go 'fore we get to Waukesha! Git *on* with ya!"

"Do you think he belongs with the band?" Martha asked.

"Wait," Caroline answered. "Something's painted on the side of his wagon. But I can't see the letters."

"Wait till the horses come up over the bridge," Martha advised.

With a cacophony of snorts, whinnies, and grunts from the horses and angry shouts from the driver, the horses and wagon finally bumped across the log bridge. "M-A-B-I-E," Caroline

268

spelled the bold black letters painted on the side of the wagon. They were followed by the letters C-I-R-C-U-S. Both words were framed in a big rectangle that was painted orange. "Does that spell circus, Martha?" Caroline stumbled over her words, she was speaking so fast. "It does! It's the Mabie Circus!"

"Oh, Caroline," Martha cried. "I hope we haven't missed it!"

As if to answer her question, the wagon was immediately followed by four majestic black horses. Thick tapestried blankets woven in blue, white, and gold were hung over their backs, their gold-fringe edges swaying back and forth as the horses clopped along proudly. Two men dressed in black, holding slender whips, walked beside each horse, blue-and-white feathers floating above their black hats.

"I think it's just the beginning!" Caroline sang out. "Look! There are some funny-looking folks behind the horses!"

"Clowns!" Martha exclaimed. "I've seen them in town on posters for the circus!"

Caroline had never seen a circus poster or

a clown before, and her mouth opened wide as the two figures marched up toward the bridge side by side. The first clown wore baggy gray trousers and a blousy white shirt that was dotted with enormous red spots. A pointed hat was slanted above his mop of curly black hair, and his face was painted white. The second figure was dressed in a shirt and multicolored trousers stitched together from rags. His face was rubbed black with charcoal, and only his painted white mouth was visible, a wide shining grin that spread from ear to ear.

"Are they ladies or gentlemen?" Caroline wondered aloud.

"They're just clowns," Martha answered. "What's the red-spotted one carrying, do you think?"

Caroline was so fascinated by the clowns, she hadn't even noticed that the one with the bright-red dots was holding a small bundle all dressed up in a flowery print dress. "It's a baby!" Caroline said. Then she shrieked in surprise when the bundle began squirming in the clown's arms and poked a pink snout out of a fold in the dress. "Oh, no, Martha! It's a baby pig," Caroline said, giggling. "And it's wearing a bonnet!"

Turning his head toward the sound of the girls' laughter, the dotted clown searched along the cattails beside the bridge, eventually spotting Caroline and Martha at the edge of the marsh. Tucking the baby pig under one arm, he nodded and waved at the girls with his other white-gloved hand.

"The clown sees us, Martha!" Caroline cried. "He's waving right at us!" Jumping up and down, Caroline waved back, laughing gleefully as the clown tried to balance across the rolling logs and wrestle with his squirmy pig at the same time.

"Jumping jackrabbits!" Martha said in hushed tones, her eyes wide with awe. "I never . . ."

Distracted from the clown, Caroline spun around to see where Martha was pointing.

A massive man with a tightly cropped beard and flat black hair was stepping up to the first log, towering over the two creamy-white steeds that followed him. He wore a sleeveless green shirt that showed off his huge arms and rippling muscles. His long legs were as wide as tree trunks, and his boots looked as big as logs.

"He must be one of those giants Mother reads about in our storybooks," Caroline whispered.

Just then a rectangular cage with wooden beams rattled and clanged toward the bridge. A big animal, all furry and white, was moving and twisting about inside the cage. "What is *that*?" Caroline asked, leaning forward for a better look.

The cage bumped and clattered over the logs, and when it was finally in full view, the animal inside flashed its furry white face, with its black nose and eyes, at Caroline and Martha. "It's a bear!" Martha exclaimed. "A white bear!"

"Whoever heard of a white bear?" Caroline asked, dumbfounded. In the forests around town she had seen black bears from a distance, and brown bears too. But never had she even heard of a white bear.

"Everyone who's ever seen a circus, I guess," Martha said.

The rattling cage was followed by a small wagon displaying a large mural on its side. Painted against a cloudless blue sky, two great pyramids jutted up from a golden field. In front of the pyramids stood a tall brown animal with an oval head and a long, slender neck that curved into a humped back. Its hind legs were taller and thicker than its spindly front legs, and its head was capped with black fuzzy hair that matched the beard puffing out beneath its square jaw. Caroline didn't know what to make of such a strange-looking animal.

"Have you ever seen one of those, Martha?" she asked, pointing at the mural.

"No," Martha admitted.

"What's that on the animal's back?"

"Looks like some sort of bump or hump or—"

"It *is* a hump, I bet!" Caroline said excitedly. "Maybe it's a camel, like the one in the

Bible verse. You know, the animal that can't fit through the eye of a needle!"

"How do you remember that, Caroline?" Martha asked with admiration, studying the man and woman crossing the bridge on the top of the wagon. "Who do you suppose they are?"

The man was dressed in white. His black eyes and brows stood out sharply against his pale ivory skin, and his hair was covered by a white cloth that was wrapped and folded around his head. Beside him sat a woman whose face was hidden by a black veil, all but her deep dark eyes.

"Maybe those big triangles behind the camel are houses and they live in them," Caroline decided. "It says E-X-O-T-I-C L-A-N-D-S under the picture. I don't know what it means."

"Me either," Martha agreed. "It must be the place where they live."

A shrill, shrieking trumpet blared through the air. Caroline's stomach flipped, and she jumped backward in the grass. A second shriek followed as a great gray beast thumped toward the bridge in smooth, rhythmic strides, swinging its wrinkly gray trunk and flapping its immense gray ears. "An elephant!" Caroline and Martha shouted at once.

When the elephant arrived at the edge of the creek, it dipped its trunk into the tumbling, bubbly water and stood perfectly still. Rolling its long nose up to its mouth, it snorted and squirted all the water it had drawn from the creek inside.

"It's drinking!" Caroline laughed delightedly.

"Move along, old gal!" A thin man walking beside the elephant called out. Pushing up his green-and-gray flannel sleeves, the man led the enormous animal to the foot of the bridge.

The elephant stepped up to the first log and raised its huge leg. Placing its enormous foot down on the log, it shifted its weight, swinging its trunk and hesitating before moving forward onto the next log.

"It's afraid of the logs!" Martha said incredulously. "That big old elephant is afraid of a bridge made of logs!"

"It's tiptoeing, Martha!" Caroline cried, watching the elephant shuffle its huge gray toes from one log to the next. "An elephant that tiptoes!"

Caroline and Martha clapped and laughed and urged the elephant forward. They were still jumping up and down on the edge of the marsh when the great gray beast stepped off the bridge, trumpeted in victory, and trotted off with a resounding *thud, thud, thud* after the circus wagons.

Carts filled with planks and folding backs, and cages occupied by playful monkeys and slithering snakes, rolled one after the other over the bridge. Caroline and Martha *ooh*ed and *ah*ed as each one passed. By the time the last wagon rolled off the bridge, Caroline's palms were red and stinging from clapping so much, and her throat felt raspy and sore.

"They must be heading straight through town if they're going to Waukesha," Martha said, reaching down into the grass and gathering her books. "We can follow them till we get to the crossroads, and then we'll have to

run the rest of the way home so we won't be late. I can't wait to tell Henry and Joseph about the circus!"

"And Eliza and Mother and Thomas," Caroline continued, wiping the dirt off her speller.

Following Martha over the corduroy bridge, Caroline balanced from one log to the next on the soles of her bare feet, stepping in the footsteps of all the animals and circus folk who had crossed the bridge only moments before. Caroline and Martha followed the circus wagons all the way through town, pausing as they reached the crossroads and had to go in a different direction.

"Oh, I wish we could follow the circus all the way to Waukesha!" Caroline sighed, cupping her hand over her eyes and watching as the clowns and the elephant, the wagons and the bear, clattered off toward the sinking sun.

White Bears

"If we fill both these buckets, Eliza, we won't have to come back for more," Caroline explained as she followed Wolf across forest paths that were speckled with sunshine. "Pick all the beechnuts and hazelnuts and acorns you can find. And anything else that you think Hog might like. He eats most everything, and we have to get him as fat as we can. Mother says butchering time's only a few months away."

"And then we'll get a new hog?" Eliza asked.

"Not till spring," Caroline answered. "Mother and Joseph will trade for a feeder then."

"We'll call it Hog too?" Eliza asked, confused.

"Every pig I can remember, Henry named Hog." Caroline shrugged. "He says he'd forget all their names if he had to think of a new one every year."

Each evening in summer and fall, Caroline and Martha spent the hour before supper in the woods, collecting buckets of nuts and berries to feed Hog. Caroline loved this chore, roaming through the forest, smelling the fresh evergreens, spying on the squirrels and rabbits scampering from sunspot to sunspot. Today Caroline was teaching Eliza how to help.

"I'm going farther up a ways, Eliza. You can gather all the feed around here," Caroline said. "Stay here with Eliza, Wolf," she ordered, petting the dog's long, furry nose.

Stepping around honey-pink petals of shooting star hanging backward on their leafless stalks and through the bunchberry blossoms

that carpeted sections of the forest, Caroline
hunted for Hog's food, singing:

> *"Can she make a cherry pie, Billy boy,*
> *   Billy boy?*
> *Can she make a cherry pie, charming*
> *   Billy?*
> *She can make a cherry pie,*
> *With a twinkle in her eye,*
> *But she's a young thing and cannot leave*
> *   her mother."*

The wooden bucket became heavier and
heavier as Caroline tossed handfuls of nuts
and berries inside. A little bit more and I'll be
done, she thought cheerfully.

A rustling of leaves and two loud thuds followed by a yelp and a hoot suddenly broke
the stillness of the hushed forest. Caroline
jumped. "Eliza?" she called, looking all around
her as Wolf's sharp barking resonated through
the trees.

"I'm over here!"

Wolf bounding along beside her, Eliza was scurrying across the forest floor. Two short curls had escaped her yellow braids and were hanging down her forehead. "What was that noise, do you suppose?" she asked fearfully.

"I don't know," Caroline said, stroking Wolf's back until he calmed down. "And I don't think we should wait to find out. My bucket's almost full. How 'bout yours?"

"Not yet," Eliza answered. "I can't go as fast as you."

"We have to fill it to the top, or Henry will give it to us good tomorrow morning when he feeds Hog," Caroline said, the pounding of her heart still thumping in her ears. "Come on. I'll help you so we'll finish lickety-split."

Together the girls rooted through the forest, searching around moss-covered tree trunks and kicking through piles of leaves and pine boughs to find more food for Hog. Caroline was pouring two more handfuls of acorns into Eliza's bucket when another yelp rang through the trees. Wolf stood tall, growling low in his throat.

Pointing straight ahead, Eliza whispered, "I saw it, Caroline. Way down there."

The last few acorns in Caroline's hand missed the bucket and plunked to the ground as she stood up and followed Eliza's gaze. "Where?" she questioned anxiously.

"There!" Eliza said.

At the very dimmest, farthest point of the forest Caroline could just barely see a white figure bounding up a tree. The next instant, a second white figure followed the first. "Get your bucket and come along, Eliza," Caroline said urgently. "Whatever they are, there are two of them."

"But it's not full." Eliza looked down. "We didn't finish filling my bucket!"

"Mine's full," Caroline said firmly, handing Eliza her bucket and lifting up her own. "It doesn't matter if yours isn't. We have to go now."

Pulling Eliza by the hand, Caroline dashed through the forest, skirting trees and stepping over twisted roots and vines that jutted up from the ground. Not once did she look back until she stepped into the soft meadow that was flooded with sunlight at the forest's edge. The climbing white figures were nowhere to be seen.

"They didn't follow us, I don't think," Caroline breathed.

"Can we stop? Please!" Eliza panted.

"For a minute," Caroline agreed. Setting her bucket on the ground, she bent over and, hands on her knees, breathed fast and deep. She glanced into her bucket to see how many acorns and nuts she had lost on her trek out of the woods, relieved to find it was still almost full. Straightening up again, she examined her sore hand, which was still stinging where she had carried the wooden handle of the bucket. Her palm was red and hot.

"Is your hand stinging and itching as bad as mine, Eliza?" Caroline asked, looking over at her little sister. Eliza's braids had come loose, and wisps of golden hair draped her pretty round face.

"It hurts some," Eliza admitted, rubbing her

hands together. "But it hurt much more when we were running through the woods."

"How's that?" Caroline asked. Then she searched the ground. "Eliza, where's your bucket?"

"The wood was digging into my fingers, and you were going so fast, and it was hurting something awful," Eliza said in a rush of words. "I let go of the bucket, Caroline! Don't be mad," she pleaded, near tears. "We can go back and get it. We can fill it up again in no time."

"Not now we can't!" Caroline snapped. "I'm not going anywhere near that forest without Henry or Joseph. Those were white bears in those trees! I'm sure as can be!"

"White bears!" Eliza exclaimed. "How do you know?"

"I saw one in a cage going over the corduroy bridge when the circus passed through town last month. Whatever was climbing those trees was big and fast and white. What else could it be but white bears?"

Eliza scrambled to her feet. "I want to go home now," she said, her voice quavering.

"Me too," Caroline said, reaching for her bucket.

Crickets clicked an evening lullaby as Caroline and Eliza crossed the meadow in silence and continued swiftly down the road to the frame house. Wolf jogged along beside them, his ears perked up and his eyes alert.

"You go on in, Eliza," Caroline said as they walked up to the house. "I have to take Hog's feed to the barn."

The door to the house banged shut as Caroline lugged her heavy bucket past the woodpile and garden and into the barn. Bathed in the soft light of early evening, the three small rooms glittered with specks of hay dust floating in the air. The barn smelled sweet and dusty, and Caroline took a deep breath, feeling happy and safe again as she stepped around piles of hay; oats and barley, scattered about the dirt floor, stuck to her bare feet. Standing on tiptoes, she slid the bucket of feed she had collected onto the lid of the grain bin and turned to hug Wolf, who was waiting at her heels.

"Good boy," she praised the dog, patting him on the head. "Be a good boy tonight, Wolf. I'll see you in the morning."

With a quick wave to Wolf, Caroline left the barn. The sun slipping from the sky in breezy strokes of color told Caroline it was time for supper, and her grumbling stomach agreed. She was skipping past the garden when a flash of white dashed by on the dirt road in front of the house. Caroline flew across the yard, burst through the door of the frame house, and slammed it shut behind her.

"For goodness' sakes!" Mother exclaimed. "What are you doing, Caroline, slamming that door like that? You near frightened me out of my shoes!"

"I'm . . . I'm sorry, Mother," Caroline said, her hand pressed against her heaving chest. "I saw the white bears! They were running loose in front of the house!"

"Caroline Lake Quiner!" Mother said incredulously. "You've never been one to make up such stories! What has gotten into you, child?"

"It's not a story, Mother," Caroline cried. "Ask Eliza! We were in the woods getting food for Hog and we heard some noises and looked and saw two white bears climbing in the trees!"

"Is this true, Eliza?" Mother asked her youngest daughter, who was at the washstand scrubbing her hands.

"Yes, ma'am," Eliza answered, nodding her head emphatically. "We saw them. Two white bears."

Mother began peeling an onion. "All the days I've lived in Wisconsin, I have never yet heard a body tell a story about seeing a white bear," she said.

"I saw a white bear that day the circus passed over the corduroy bridge," Martha spoke up from the table she was busy setting. "Caroline saw it too."

"A white bear in a cage, perhaps," Mother agreed. "But there aren't any running free in the forests, Martha. Whatever it was you saw,

Caroline," Mother firmly assured her, "it wasn't a white bear. I'm as certain of that as I am that the sun will rise in the morning."

"They weren't just in the woods, Mother," Caroline persisted. "When I was coming from the barn just now, I saw them running down the road right in front of our house!"

"How could you see anything in front of the house when you were all the way back at the barn?" Mother asked. "And the day just shy of twilight, no less. Your eyes were playing tricks on you, Caroline. Now wash up, and not another word about white bears. You're scaring your little sister, and your baby brother can surely hear your tale from the other room as well. I'll not have a pack of sleepless children under my roof tonight!"

Joseph and Henry burst through the door as the rest of the family was sitting down to supper. "Charlie says his mother sends her greetings," Henry relayed his friend's message as he dipped his hands into the washbowl, rubbed them together, and then dried them with a quick pat on his brown trousers.

Mother shook her head. "No sense drying clean hands on dirty trousers, Henry. Next time use the rag by the washstand to dry up."

"Yes, ma'am," Henry said, hopping into his chair.

Caroline pushed cold beans around her plate, nibbled at her squash and onions, and swallowed a small bite of bread and three sips of milk. She didn't speak about the white bears or anything else while she dried the dishes and returned them to the dish dresser. She was even quiet as she stitched absentmindedly on her sampler and pulled on her nightgown before bed.

When the girls finally settled down for the night, Caroline waited until Mother started singing in her rocking chair down below and Eliza's soft breaths sounded deep and steady. Then she sat up on her elbows and whispered, "Martha? Are you asleep?"

"Yes," Martha murmured sleepily. "Why aren't you?"

"I know it was white bears climbing those trees and running in front of our house today,"

Caroline said, trying to keep her voice hushed. "I saw them with my own eyes."

"In a dark forest, Caroline," Martha answered with a yawn, "it could have been something else. Just like Mother said."

"Like what?"

"Like an owl."

"Too small," Caroline disagreed.

"Like a fox."

"Foxes are red," Caroline disagreed again.

Rolling over, Martha sighed in exasperation. "Well then, I can't figure what you saw any better than you!"

"It was a white bear!" Caroline whispered determinedly. "Two white bears. They must have run away from a circus."

"The circus folk would have come after them, Caroline," Martha reasoned. "And besides, what difference does it make now? You're not in the forest, so why worry about them anyway?"

"Maybe they followed us home," Caroline whispered the dreadful thought she'd been thinking all evening. "Who's to say they won't climb right up our oak tree and into our window while we're sleeping?"

"That is the silliest thing I ever heard you think up, Caroline!" Martha said. "Now go to sleep or I'll tell Mother you're talking about those bears again."

Settling back on the mattress, Caroline rested her cheek on her pillow and gazed across the room. The full moon cast a white glow over the darkness, silhouetting the old oak's leafy branches. The leaves were still, and except for the occasional cry of a wolf far off in the distance and the endless chatter of the crickets, the night was still.

Restlessly Caroline rolled over so she wouldn't be able to see the window anymore. She closed her eyes and began reciting her prayers over and over to herself:

> "*Now I lay me down to sleep,*
> *I pray the Lord my soul to keep.*
> *If I should die before I wake,*
> *I pray the Lord my soul to take.*
> *If I should die before I wake,*

*I pray the Lord my soul to take.
If I should die . . ."*

Flipping over on her back, Caroline stared up at the darkness. She didn't want to die, and she didn't want the Lord to take her soul, either. Counting numbers in her head, she reached all the way to two hundred and sixty-eight, but she was still awake. Rolling over on her stomach and wiggling her foot back and forth, Caroline spelled all her vocabulary words for this week, and last week, and the week before, to no avail. She turned on her side, stared at the window, and turned over again. Through the night Caroline tossed and turned.

The once-dark room was dimly lit when Caroline climbed wearily out of bed. Her head was throbbing as she opened the middle drawer of the chest and felt around for her dress and petticoats.

"Goodness glory! What are you doing up so early, Caroline?" Mother asked as Caroline stepped off the last stair and crossed the wood-plank floor to the hearth. "Heavens, child! Are you sick? Your eyes are more red than a rooster's!"

"I wanted to get my chores done early, is all," Caroline said. Without even stopping to smell the hotcake batter that Mother was preparing, she walked to the washstand, scooped a handful of water from the washbasin, and splashed it over her face. The water felt cool and refreshing, but it did nothing to ease the ache behind her eyes.

"Well, you'll certainly have enough time to feed the chickens before breakfast," Mother said, watching Caroline closely. "Joseph just filled the washbasin and went back out to the woodpile. I expect Henry's out in the barn feeding Hog. You all should come back inside for breakfast once you've finished feeding the chickens, Caroline. I'll tighten your braid then."

"Yes, ma'am," Caroline answered, her mouth drying up as Mother's words, *Henry's out in the barn feeding Hog*, resounded in her ears. Bowing her head to avoid Mother's questioning gaze, Caroline fled through the door without another word.

Without so much as a wave to Joseph, Caroline dashed through the dewy grass all the way to the barn, and stopped out of breath in the middle of it. Henry was standing beside the grain bin, sweeping up some stray acorns and beechnuts that were strewn about an empty bucket.

"What are you doing here so early?" Henry asked, his sleepy blue eyes filled with surprise. "Don't your hens usually have to wait till after you eat your breakfast to get theirs?"

"Yes, but . . ." Caroline began.

"Oh, I only found one bucket of feed for Hog on the grain bin this morning," Henry continued. "Where's the other one? I've 'bout combed through every pile of hay in this barn looking for it."

"It's still in the woods, Henry," Caroline whispered, staring at the dirt floor as her cheeks grew hot with shame.

"In the woods?" Henry asked, tousling his already tousled hair. "I don't understand, little Brownbraid. Why collect a bucket of Hog's feed and leave it sitting in the woods?"

"Eliza left it," Caroline said. "It wasn't her fault. We were running out of the forest as fast as we could."

"Running?" Henry asked. "From what?"

Caroline's voice grew louder and her words tumbled out so quickly, Henry could barely understand what she was saying. "From the white bears!" she cried. "They got loose from the circus and were climbing some trees in the woods, and we saw them and ran as fast as we could to get away. They followed us all the way home!"

"Whoa!" Henry hollered, his forehead wrinkling with concern as he dropped his broom with a thud and took firm hold of his sister's shoulders. "Stop right there 'fore you make yourself sick, Caroline! Are you talking about the woods out back of Mrs. Stoddard's?"

Unable to speak, Caroline nodded her head.

"Right after school, before supper?" Henry questioned.

"Yes," Caroline squeaked out.

"Well, that story just doesn't make any

sense," Henry said. "I was in that very same forest with Charlie yesterday. We were climbing all sorts of trees, and neither one of us saw any white bears!"

"They ran past the house last night, right before supper, Henry," Caroline told him earnestly. "I saw them right after I left Hog's bucket in the barn."

Henry looked at Caroline for a moment, his eyes puzzled. Suddenly the wrinkles on his brow disappeared, his eyes lit up, and he tossed his head back, yelping with laughter that filled the morning air.

"What's so funny?" Caroline called out as Henry wrapped his arms around his stomach and howled even louder.

"The white bears!" Henry gulped for air. "Don't you see? The white bears were me and Charlie!"

"Don't you laugh at me, Henry Quiner," Caroline snapped.

"I'm not laughing at you," Henry chortled, unable to stop. "It was us! We were climbing trees and fooling around in those very same woods last night. We were the ones you saw running past the house, too!"

"You and Charlie don't look anything like white bears!" Caroline shouted back at her brother.

"Last night we did," Henry answered, taking extra-deep breaths between chuckles as he tried to calm himself down. "We took off all our clothes, save our long underwear, so we wouldn't tear them when we were climbing in the trees."

"It was *you*?" Caroline asked, weak with relief.

"*I'm* your white bear, little Brownbraid." Henry grinned. "Me and Charlie, that is. Maybe we should join us a circus and dance around in our underwear!"

Caroline rubbed her eyes wearily, trying to make sense of it all. "I'd better go for the bucket Eliza left in the forest, so you can feed Hog," she finally said.

"He's got enough here to get him through breakfast, that big old pig," Henry joked. "I'll go get the bucket while you're off at school.

You just hurry and feed your chickens now, Caroline, so you won't be late getting back for Mother's hotcakes. You know how she waits till everyone's at the table to eat, and I'm so hungry this morning, I don't want her holding breakfast for anybody!"

Her head was still aching and her eyes stung with fatigue, but Caroline filled her bucket with grain and scattered it about her squawking feathered friends quickly and cheerfully. Henry worked in the barn at a smattering of chores until Caroline finished, and together they walked back to the frame house for breakfast.

"I'm so hungry, I could eat a whole stack of hotcakes!" Caroline exclaimed as she neared the house and smelled the sweet aroma of Mother's hotcakes escaping through the open back door.

"I'm so hungry, I could eat a bear," Henry quipped, dropping his arm around Caroline's shoulder. "But not a white bear, of course!"

"Of course!" Caroline giggled, and followed her brother into the house.

Letters

The full harvest moon seemed to linger in the sky night after night, pouring bright white light upon the earth. Days shortened and the air grew crisp. The last ears of corn had been pulled from their dry brown stalks, and only the squash and pumpkins, still hugging their twisted vines, splashed the garden with color. The root cellar, empty all summer, brimmed with crocks of vegetables, berries, fruits, and preserves. Bundles of herbs, some still green, hung upside down from the ceiling to dry. The cellar smelled sweet and spicy all at once.

Early one morning, the air outside the frame house pulsed with a low, steady rumble. Even before she looked out the window, Caroline knew the pigeons had arrived. Twice a year she heard the familiar low-pitched hum and rustle of passenger pigeons. The sky was suddenly darkened by millions of birds, flapping their wings and gliding together in an endless throng, to the north in the spring, and to the south in the fall.

Descending from the skies in great flapping flocks, the pigeons stripped the woods, fields, and trees in Brookfield of the seeds, grain, berries, and wild nuts that hadn't yet been harvested. Each day of the pigeons' flight, Henry and Joseph left the house carrying long, heavy sticks and spent hours with all the men and boys in town trapping and killing the pigeons. Caroline and Martha stayed home, doing all but the hardest of their brothers' chores as well as their own. Supper and dinner were much quieter than usual, and there was no noisy competition between Henry and

Joseph at the checkerboard before bedtime.
The boys spent the night with Charlie and
Mr. Carpenter, hunting birds by the flaming
light of torches and sulfur that they burned
beneath the trees. The frame house remained
quiet and lonely until Joseph and Henry
returned before first light. They slept for a
few hours, then headed down the stairs for
breakfast, weary but excited.

On the final morning of the hunt, Henry
was exuberant. "Mr. Ben says this is the finest
haul he can remember," he exclaimed. "He
told us the wagons shipping birds to Chicago
are loaded with barrels that can hold some
forty-four dozen birds each. Between Joseph
and me, we caught enough birds to fill one of
those barrels by ourselves! And Mr. Carleton's
paying top dollar for the pigeons. Two whole
cents a bird! Do you know what that means,
Mother?" Henry asked, his face glowing.
"That means we're going to bring us home
more than ten whole dollars!"

"I can think of many more pleasant ways
to earn money than slaughtering all those

birds," Mother remarked as she filled Thomas's cup with milk.

"But *ten* dollars, Mother!" Henry protested. "We made ten dollars. That's almost rich!"

"Better to be rich in good works, Henry-O," Mother advised, taking her seat at the table. "Never mind. You and Joseph have worked hard these last few days, and your father would have been proud of you."

"Thomas is proud too!" Thomas grinned and pounded his little fist on the table.

"I don't understand how you can hunt so many birds all at once," Caroline admitted, spreading some butter on her hotcakes.

"It's not really like hunting," Joseph explained. "It's much easier because everywhere you look, you see pigeons. They're all over the forests and the meadows, eating whatever they find. We set traps with our nets to catch the birds, or sometimes we just step up behind them while they're eating and hit them with our sticks. This year, so many birds landed, we mostly just had to knock them dead out of the trees."

"Joseph," Mother said, "please stop such chatter at the breakfast table."

"But that's not even the worst of it, Mother," Henry said. "Some boys, like Danny McCarthy for one, stick poles in the ground and tie their dead pigeons to them. When other pigeons come and flock around the dead one on the pole, Danny and his friends, they lay in wait and get those birds too! And they use shotguns to kill 'em! *Boom! Boom, boom!*" Henry cried, shooting at an imaginary target.

Mother said sternly, "Henry-O! Not another word, please!" as Caroline's fork clattered to her plate. She looked down at her steaming hotcakes, at the butter and sugar syrup slipping down the sides of the stack in a creamy brown-and-white stream. She had eaten only three forkfuls of the rich brown cakes, but suddenly she couldn't eat another bite.

"I've heard all I care to about the passenger pigeons," Mother said calmly. "I only hope you've saved enough birds for me to make a pigeon pie. I'd also like to make some soup, and preserve one or two in the cellar."

"There are half a dozen in the barn at least, and Mr. Ben says he'll take care of the rest for us," Joseph said. "We weren't sure what you wanted us to do with the pigeons we kept, so we left them in the barn for safekeeping."

"We'll start by plucking them," Mother said, her mood brightening. "We should begin first thing after our morning chores. I have a sack of goose feathers started that's not yet full enough to make into a pillow. We can add the pigeon feathers to the goose down. I reckon it won't do any harm to mix the feathers, and we'll have us a new pillow!"

"For me!" Thomas said, his mouth full of hotcakes.

"May I please say one more thing?" Henry looked at Mother sheepishly. "Not about the birds, I promise."

"Yes?" Mother eyed Henry.

Henry spoke slowly so as not to confuse his words. "Last night Mr. Ben told me that Mrs. Carpenter told him that Mr. Porter told her that there's some letters come for you at the general store. I'm setting Hog loose in town

this morning to fatten him up on bird car-
casses—"

"Henry-O," Mother warned.

"—and I could fetch your letters at the same
time," Henry finished, his eyes lighting up.
"Kill two birds with one stone." He chuckled
to himself at his joke, but Mother didn't seem
to notice.

"You'll have your hands full just keeping
Hog in line, Henry-O," Mother said, thinking
aloud. "Martha can begin the crust for the
pigeon pie while Joseph, Eliza, and I pluck
and clean the pigeons. That leaves Caroline
to look after Thomas. They both can go along
with you, Henry, and get the letters from the
general store."

"You're going to let Caroline fetch something so important, Mother?" Martha asked
incredulously. "She's only seven years old!"

"Caroline knows the value of a letter,
Martha," Mother said dryly. "I expect she'll
have little trouble in picking them up and bringing them home safely. Am I correct, Caroline?"

"Yes, ma'am." Caroline nodded importantly, with a sideways glance at Martha. "I'll be very careful."

As soon as the frame house was swept and tidied, Caroline took hold of Thomas's hand.

"You stay with your sister, Thomas. No running off," Mother instructed. "Be mindful of your little brother's whereabouts, Caroline."

"I will, ma'am," Caroline promised as she led Thomas outside. The cool morning breeze blew the folds of Caroline's apron across her brown woolen skirt, and she shivered even though she was wearing her heaviest long-sleeve dress. Looking up at the clear blue sky, Caroline listened to the soft sounds of the morning. "Seems the pigeons have gone away just as quick and sudden as they came," she said.

"Where'd they go?" Thomas asked, squinting into the bright sunshine.

"Mother says they go south this time of year," Caroline answered. "But I'm not certain where south is."

"This way, Hog, move it!" Henry was shouting as he ran around the side of the house, Wolf trotting along behind. "Let's go." He waved to his brother and sister.

Caroline, Thomas, and Wolf crunched along the leaf-covered road behind Henry and their enormous pig. Every few steps, Hog wandered off to poke his snout into a pile of leaves or a clump of roadside flowers, sniffing for food. Henry tapped his silvery back with the crooked end of a long stick, ordering, "Keep over this a ways, Hog. There's plenty of feed for you in town."

Holding Thomas's fingers tightly, Caroline followed along, giggling at the sight of Hog's wrinkled, fleshy backside waddling here and there while Henry tried to hurry him along.

As they neared the crossroads of town, the road suddenly grew crowded with men and boys driving their hogs toward the wagons that were lined up in front of shops and houses on the main road. Most of the pigs were busy eating the pigeon remains scattered about and tossed in heaps at the sides of wagons. An

occasional clamor of "Stop!" "Wait!" or
"Come here!" erupted, and all heads turned
to watch one of the owners dash after a squeal-
ing hog that whizzed away in a gray flash.

"Don't get any such ideas in that big fat head
of yours, Hog," Henry warned, holding his stick
close to Hog's side as he watched the chaos.
"We'll get a little closer to the wagons, and you
can stand there and eat whatever you want."

"They're eating up the birds!" Thomas
exclaimed in wonder, pointing at the enormous
pigs chewing dead birds all around him.

Feeling queasy, Caroline looked at Henry.
"I'm going for Mother's letters now," she told
him.

"Watch your step," Henry said as he prod-
ded Hog along.

For the first time that morning Caroline
wished she had stayed at home to pluck pigeon
feathers instead of going to town. She held
her breath and hurried Thomas through the
littered, smelly road, past the wagons that were
heaped with dead pigeons, and into the general store.

"Well, good morning to you, Miss Quiner!" the storekeeper greeted Caroline as she closed the door behind her with a great sigh of relief and breathed in all the spices. "And to you too, lad," he added, nodding his shiny bald head at Thomas.

"Good morning, Mr. Porter." Caroline tipped her face up to address the tall man. "Mother sent us to fetch some letters for her, sir. Mrs. Carpenter sent word that they had come."

"Ah, yes." Mr. Porter smiled, setting his pencil down on the counter. "One came a few days ago, I believe, and one arrived just yesterday. I'll get them for you right away."

While Mr. Porter searched for the letters, Caroline gazed up and down the shelves that were stacked with goods. Her eyes rested on the two glass jars that held glistening sticks of peppermint and round wintergreen candies.

"I want one," Thomas said longingly, his eyes fixed on the very same jars.

"Me too," Caroline whispered, tousling his thick brown hair. "But we can't have any."

"Why?" Thomas questioned.

"Because they don't belong to us," Caroline answered, feeling very grown up. "And they cost money, besides. Now shush, Thomas."

"Here you are, young lady." Mr. Porter turned back to them, sliding two thin brown envelopes over the edge of the crowded counter. "It looks like the one on top has traveled all the way from back East."

"Thank you, sir," Caroline said excitedly, taking the letters from the grocer and examining the sprawling black script on the top envelope. The letters were curvy and connected, and she couldn't read one word.

"You be sure and send my greetings to your Mother." Mr. Porter smiled down at her, pots and pans sparkling above his head. "Tell her I'll add the postage to her account."

"I will," Caroline promised. "Thank you, sir, and good-bye."

" 'Bye!" Thomas echoed.

Hog was still busily feasting when Caroline and Thomas ran up to Henry. "Here they are," she exclaimed, waving the letters in front of him. "Mr. Porter says one of them's from back East, but I can't make sense of any of the words on it."

"Bring it on home, Caroline," Henry instructed. "No sense in my taking Hog away from all this food. Tell Mother I'll be along by dinner."

"Come now, Thomas," Caroline urged. She couldn't wait to get home and learn more about the mysterious letters. With a quick good-bye to Henry, Caroline took Thomas's hand and started back to the frame house, the letters clasped tightly in her hand.

Thomas hurried along behind Caroline, trying his best to keep up. When they arrived at the frame house, Mother was alone at the table, placing the top crust over a pigeon pie. "Goodness, Thomas, your cheeks are as round and red as apples!" She smiled, looking up from her work.

"Caroline goes fast," Thomas complained. "I go fast too!" he added proudly, looking at the pie. "Now eat!"

"Soon," Mother promised, turning her attention to Caroline. "Did you get the letters?" she asked.

"Yes, Mother." Caroline smiled proudly. "They're right here, safe and sound!"

"Good for you, Caroline," Mother praised, rubbing her hands on her apron and wiping away the flour and dough stuck between her fingers. "I can hardly wait to see who's sent them."

"I go outside!" Thomas said, bouncing up and down in place.

"Go ahead," Mother agreed. "But don't go any farther than the barn."

"Mr. Porter says this one is from back East," Caroline said as she handed it to Mother. "And here's the other letter too."

"He's right," Mother said, scanning the writing on the first envelope as she set the second letter down on the table. "But it's not from Boston. I only hope it isn't . . . Well, let's just see what's inside."

Sliding a knife through the edge of the envelope, Mother pulled out a single sheet of paper.

With the help of the firelight, Caroline could see that the same heavy black script on the envelope filled the front of the paper that Mother was reading. "Who is it from?" she asked eagerly.

Mother didn't answer. Her eyes darted from one line to the next, and as she read, she slowly lifted her fingertips to her trembling lips. Despite her best attempts to conceal her expression, Mother's face grew terribly troubled.

"Please, Mother," Caroline asked as fear crept up inside her. "What's happened?"

"Oh, Caroline!" Mother said, her voice breaking as she folded the letter and stuffed it back into the envelope. "You mustn't worry." She tried to smile down at Caroline as she wiped the corners of her eyes. "It's not a matter that concerns you at this time. So run along to the barn and see if Joseph and Martha have finished with the pigeons. If not, you can help them, since dinner's not quite ready yet."

Caroline knew she shouldn't ask any more questions, but she had no choice. Mother had the very same look of fear and worry on her face that Caroline had seen only once before, the day Uncle Elisha had arrived with news about Father's shipwreck. "Please, Mother," Caroline begged, "say what's wrong!"

Mother was silent for a moment; then she knelt down in front of Caroline. Her hands were cold and shaking when she took hold of Caroline's hands. "I suppose I'll have to tell you soon enough," Mother said. "But I don't want you to breathe a word of this to your brothers and sisters until I tell them also."

"Yes, ma'am," Caroline said.

"We are going to have to leave our house, Caroline," Mother said, searching Caroline's face with her own troubled eyes.

"I don't understand," Caroline said, fear squeezing her breath away.

"Years ago . . . you weren't even yet three years old, I don't think," Mother began, "your father and I fell on some very hard times. We were forced to sell our land, and a friend of Father's, Mr. Michael Woods, who lived here in Brookfield, bought it. Mr. Woods didn't have any intention of living on the land, so he kindly let us remain here for a small amount of money. Even after he and his wife moved back to Pennsylvania, Mr. Woods never asked us to leave, but your father and I knew he'd want to reclaim the property someday for himself or his kin. This is from Mr. Woods." Mother held the letter up in front of Caroline. "His sister and her family are coming to Brookfield this spring. They plan to live on this land. We'll have to find another place to live."

Caroline looked at the piece of folded paper, so close to her face. She wanted nothing more than to tear it into tiny pieces and make sure that what Mother was telling her would not come true.

"You mustn't worry, Caroline," Mother said, sounding determined. "I've been planning for this day, taking on extra sewing jobs from folks in town and saving the money so we can buy land somewhere else."

"In Brookfield?" Caroline asked, not knowing whether to cry or shout or kick the leg of the table, but wanting to do all three at once.

"Well, we need enough land to raise a good

crop and some livestock," Mother said. "I don't imagine that we can get that kind of land in Brookfield for the amount of money I'm able to pay."

Caroline dropped her head. She thought about Anna and Elsa, about the Carpenters, and about Mrs. Stoddard. Her thoughts raced as she imagined the little white church that Father had helped build, the shelves she loved to explore in the general store, the bubbling creek where she had collected buckets of berries and wildflower bouquets. She imagined the barn that had been her very first home, her bedroom and all the small, cozy rooms of their little frame house. Shutting her eyes as tightly as she could, Caroline tried to think and understand, but all she could do was cry.

"Dear Caroline," Mother said, pulling her into a warm hug, "you mustn't cry! We don't have to go anywhere until spring. That's six whole months from now! Who knows what might happen by then?" she added cheerfully, smiling down at Caroline through her own tears. "The good Lord has always taken care of us. He's not about to stop now. Now promise me, not a word about this to anyone until I've told them myself. Promise me."

"I promise," Caroline whispered.

Caroline hardly spoke during dinner and supper, and remained quiet as she embroidered at the sewing table with Mother and her sisters in the evening hour before bedtime.

Martha hummed as she clicked her knitting needles together, and Eliza carefully watched Mother's expert stitches so she could later practice similar stitches on her own piece of linen.

Joseph was stoking the fire, and Henry was sitting cross-legged on the floor in front of the hearth, whistling as he whittled away at a block of wood.

"Henry-O," Mother warned, "I've told you time and again. It's impolite to whistle in the house. Save your whistling for the outdoors, please."

"Sorry, Mother," Henry said, and began humming along with Martha.

Suddenly Martha stopped humming. "Who were the letters from today, Mother?" she asked. "You never told us at supper."

Caroline studied the verse she was stitching on her sampler. She didn't dare look up, or someone might see in her eyes that she knew Mother's secret.

"One was from Pennsylvania," Mother answered. "From a man named Michael Woods. It wasn't good news."

Joseph stopped poking the fire and turned away from the hearth. "What's happened, Mother?"

Setting her needle and fabric down, Mother glanced around the room at each expectant face. In a calm and steady voice, she recounted the contents of the letter.

"You mean we have to go away from here?" Martha asked, dropping her knitting needles on her lap as Mother finished her tale.

"Yes, Martha," Mother said. "And I don't yet know where we'll go. I have saved some money to buy land, but if we choose to purchase it from someone hereabouts, we'll likely get too little to farm and raise animals. We may need to go farther west. Land will be cheaper there."

Martha stuttered, "But how can we leave . . ."

"Charlie?" Henry finished his sister's sentence, his eyes twinkling with excitement. "Oh, Martha! It doesn't matter where our diggings are! Charlie and his folks will come visit. Heck, they might even move along with us, it's such an adventure!"

"There's the money we made from the pigeons, Mother," Joseph said. "Mr. Carleton owes us ten dollars and fifty-six cents. It could help buy more land."

"You bet!" Henry agreed.

"Thank you, boys," Mother said proudly.

"I don't have money," Thomas burst out from the settle, where he was stacking his wooden blocks.

"Well, I don't have much either." Mother laughed. "So wherever we go, it will have to be a place where we can get a fair amount of land for a good price."

"When will we go?" Eliza asked, uncertain if Mother's news was good or bad.

"In the spring," Mother replied. "I hope to get us settled soon after the sap starts to flow, Eliza. But enough questions, children!" Mother lightened her tone, trying to be cheerful. "And enough of the glum faces. Henry-O is right. We should think of this as an adventure. A chance to start over with our own land, land that can't be taken away. We'll plant wheat as well as corn, and eventually raise our own live-stock. You're all getting old enough to help with such big and important chores."

"We could raise some geese," Joseph spoke up.

"That's a fine idea!" Mother exclaimed.

"Don't forget chickens," Eliza chimed in.

"And bees! We could raise us some bees and eat all their honey!" Henry said gleefully.

"I like honey!" Thomas shouted.

"Maybe they won't have a schoolhouse in this new place." Martha grinned. "And we'll never have to go back to school!"

"Then you'll have all your lessons with me, in the new cabin that we build," Mother countered slyly.

"I hope there's a school," Caroline finally spoke up. She was happy that Mother's secret was out, but not at all excited about leaving her home and friends, the way everybody else suddenly seemed to be.

"I hope so too, Caroline," Mother agreed. "And now I do have some happier news. The other letter was from Grandma. She writes that if all goes as planned, she and Uncle Elisha's family are coming to stay with us for Christmas Eve and Christmas Day!"

"Grandma!" Caroline exclaimed. She had all but forgotten the second letter the storekeeper had given her, but now that letter was bringing her the happiest news of the day.

"How long till she comes?" Martha asked.

"Two months, give or take a week." Mother laughed. "Such a treat to have visitors for Christmas!"

Dropping her sampler on the table, Caroline

jumped up and spun around the room delightedly with Eliza and Martha. It was more than a year since Grandma had gone to Milwaukee, and though she had hoped to return to Brookfield for a visit last spring, illness and Uncle Elisha's busy job at the newspaper had kept her from traveling. But soon Grandma was coming back to the frame house, and Caroline couldn't be more excited. Grandma would understand why Caroline didn't want to leave her home.

Two more months! Caroline began counting the days.

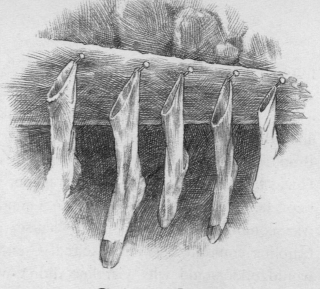

Santeclaus

The fire in the hearth blazed and popped mightily on Christmas Eve, warming the little frame house and adding a smoky aroma to the delicious scents of the gingerbread, spice cookies, and crusty brown bread that Mother had baked. Caroline rubbed a small circle of frost from the windowpane and peeked out. The world was still beneath its white winter cloak. Nothing was visible except the round, fluffy snowflakes that fell heavily from the gray winter sky.

"Do you think Uncle Elisha will still come

in all this snow?" Caroline asked Eliza as her little sister squeezed in beside her.

"I hope so," Eliza said, pressing her nose up against the glass.

The door flew open, and a huge oak log, caked with snow and chunks of ice, rolled into the room. Joseph and Henry followed, pushing both ends of the log across the room with their snowy boots. "Here it is, Mother," Henry cried. "Is it big enough?"

Mother turned from the table where she was crimping the edge of a mince pie in a dainty scalloped pattern. "It looks like it's big enough to burn for the full twelve days of Christmas." She laughed. "Good work, boys! Shut the door and try not to make too much of a mess getting it to the hearth."

"Surely you wouldn't close the door on a man bearing gifts!" Mr. Carpenter called out, poking his grinning face through the open door.

"Mr. Ben!" a chorus of voices greeted him as he stomped into the house, shutting the door behind him.

Hunching his shoulders and shivering dramatically, Mr. Carpenter exclaimed, "Whirling whippoorwills! If this snow keeps up, we'll be living in one enormous snowbank before the end of the year! We'll all have to pull on our bear coats and hibernate till spring!"

"I don't have a bear coat," Thomas said very seriously.

"Then I'll have to go find me a grizzly, and have him make one for you, little Thomas," Mr. Carpenter joked, tousling Thomas's hair. "Size, extra small!"

"Such silly stories for little ears." Mother greeted her neighbor with a warm smile. "Happy Christmas Eve, Benjamin."

"Christmas greetings to you, Charlotte," Mr. Carpenter said. "Come daybreak we're heading out to Waukesha to spend the day with Sarah's folks, so she's sent me out with the plum pudding a day early." Working his way through a crowd of children, he carefully placed a large, heavy bowl on the table. "I hope you'll enjoy every bite!"

"It's become one of our favorite Christmas

traditions!" Mother said graciously. "Thank you, Benjamin. And Sarah, too."

Tugging on Mr. Ben's trousers, Eliza looked up at him and asked quietly, "Will you still bring Christmas pudding to our new house, Mr. Ben?"

"What new house is that, little one?" Mr. Carpenter asked, kneeling down in front of Eliza and smiling into her bright eyes.

"Mother says we have to go away in the spring," Eliza explained.

Mr. Carpenter looked over at Mother, standing up quickly. "What's this, Charlotte?"

Trying her best to keep her smile bright, Mother told her neighbor the news. "Forgive me, Benjamin, for not telling you and Sarah sooner," she finished. "We've known about it for some time now, but with the harvest and butchering and smoking all the meat for winter, there never seemed to be a moment to speak to you about such things."

"Me and the Mrs. have plenty of land just down the road, Charlotte," Mr. Carpenter said without pause. "We could easily build another house on it, and build it far enough from our'n that we'd never have to bother each other. Unless we wanted to, of course."

"Thank you, Benjamin," Mother said. "But who knows how long you and Sarah will stay here? We need to put down roots on our own land and stay as long as we like without fearing that someday we'll have to leave. I've lived with that fear most every day since Henry was lost to us. Now I want some peace."

Mr. Carpenter slowly nodded, stroking his trim beard. "So where to, then?"

"I don't know yet," Mother admitted. "Somewhere we can get enough land to raise crops and livestock and keep the family eating. The boys are old enough to help care for such a place now. Since we don't have a lot of money, I imagine we will have to go farther west."

"Nonsense," Mr. Carpenter said. "It would be too hard on you and the children without Henry, Charlotte. You'd best wait and see where the government is trying to sell off land quick to raise funds for public works. That's where you're bound to get real value."

"Public works?" Joseph asked.

"Dams, bridges, canals, maybe a school or a college," Mr. Carpenter explained. "The government needs money to build all sorts of things, and one of the easiest ways they can get it is to sell off pieces of their land, fast and cheap. I'll look into it, if you like, Charlotte," he offered kindly. "Maybe we can somehow keep the Quiners close to Brookfield. I know three of your neighbors would like nothing more!"

Mother smiled. "Thank you, Benjamin. Nor would we."

For the first time in months, Caroline felt better. Mr. Ben knew their secret now, and he would help them find a place to live, Caroline just knew it. Maybe a place that wasn't so far away, after all.

The merry jingle of sleigh bells tinkled far off in the distance, growing louder and louder outside the frame house. Caroline dashed to the window and rubbed her peephole clear of frost again. "It's a bobsled, Mother!" she cried. "I can hardly see any faces beneath all the blankets and furs, but it's Grandma and Uncle Elisha, I think!"

"Will you stay, Benjamin?" Mother asked. "You could return home and bring Sarah and Charlie back with you for supper."

"A perfect idea!" Martha nodded enthusiastically.

"I think not, Charlotte," Mr. Carpenter replied, buttoning his coat and pulling his collar up around his neck and ears. "You haven't seen Henry's folks for a long time, if I'm not mistaken. Spend Christmas Eve with them, and we'll all sup together in the New Year. Now let's see." He grinned, spreading his arms wide open and counting heads. "I need four Christmas hugs and two Christmas handshakes before I head out and brave all those buckets of snow someone keeps dumping from heaven!"

Caroline waited her turn, and when Mr. Carpenter pulled her into his arms, she rested her head against the damp fur of his coat, hugging him tight.

"Happy Christmas, little Brownbraid," he whispered.

"Happy Christmas, Mr. Ben."

Mr. Carpenter left the frame house with a loud, cheerful greeting to the visitors, who, heads bowed against the falling snow, were making their way inside. "Grandma!" Caroline cried, running to hug Grandma the moment she stepped through the door, before she even had a chance to unwrap her scarf.

"Dear Caroline," Grandma said, hugging her close. "How good to be home with you again."

Caroline nodded, holding Grandma tight and feeling Christmas happiness fill her up.

Uncle Elisha and his wife were standing by the door, surrounded by Caroline's cousins, William, George Henry, and John. Bundled up so warm and tight in furs, scarves, robes, hats, mittens, and veils, they looked like a family of bears. Mother and Martha quickly took the bowls and platters that Uncle Elisha was balancing in his arms and set them on the table. The boys dropped their coats, stomped the snow off their boots, and ran to the hearth to begin their checkers matches with Henry and Joseph.

"How wonderful to see you all again!" Mother's eyes twinkled as she greeted her guests. "Mother Quiner, welcome back!"

As Mother hugged Grandma, Martha tugged on Caroline's sleeve. "I have to show you something," she whispered.

Caroline followed Martha across the room and glanced at the table that was suddenly crowded with bowls and platters and crocks. "Did you ever imagine so much food?" Martha asked incredulously. "On our table?"

"Shortbreads and stuffing, Grandma's sweet potatoes and baked apples." Caroline pointed from platter to bowl. "Mince pie and plum pudding, Mother's Christmas bread, and a goose!" she exclaimed. "A whole big wonderful goose!"

"Three big wonderful geese!" Uncle Elisha laughed from behind them. "We brought along two more for your mother to store in the cellar. They'll be a nice treat in the winter months."

"Yes, sir, thank you," Caroline said politely as she turned to face her uncle. He was smiling down at her, and as she looked at him,

Caroline noticed for the first time that Uncle Elisha looked like Father. His brown hair was dusted with gray and was much shorter than Father's, his eyes were dark brown instead of blue, and he had a neatly trimmed mustache that curled at the tips instead of the cropped beard and mustache that Father had always worn. And yet when he laughed, his cheeks flushed a bright red and his eyes crinkled up at the corners, just like Father's.

"I'm so pleased to see you again, Caroline and Martha," Uncle Elisha was saying. "You've grown up just fine! Your father would have been very proud of you."

"Thank you, Uncle Elisha," Caroline and Martha said.

"Elisha," Grandma called gently, "Charlotte has something she'd like to speak with you about. Come along now, girls. Mother says we must set the table for dinner."

"I'll be back in a moment," Uncle Elisha said with a wink.

"He's nice, I think," Caroline said reluctantly as she crossed to the dishstand with Martha.

"I never liked him before," she admitted.

"That's only because he always came at the awfulest times," Martha said. "I like him now too. I just wish he had some girls to bring to our house instead of all those boys."

Grandma cleared all the food that was to wait for Christmas Day dinner, and Caroline immediately began setting the table.

"Run along and help Thomas wash up for dinner please, Eliza." Mother's voice resounded firmly from the corner of the room behind Caroline. "Of course it's a fine idea, but I'm afraid it would be far too costly to move the family to Milwaukee, Elisha," she continued as Eliza ran off in search of Thomas.

Setting each plate and utensil down on the table as quietly as possible, Caroline listened to every word of Mother's conversation, though she knew she shouldn't.

"But what alternatives do you have, Charlotte?" Uncle Elisha asked. "The children will be near family, at least. You can work at your craft, and need stay with us only until

334

you have saved enough money to buy land nearby."

"You're more than kind to offer, but I am determined to buy our own homestead as soon as possible," Mother said resolutely. "Our neighbor says it may be possible to buy land inexpensively through some sort of public-works sale. Have you heard of such a thing?"

"Of course. Our newspaper lists such sales whenever they become public. In fact, if I'm not mistaken"—Uncle Elisha's speech quickened with excitement—"there's about to be one such sale in Jefferson County. It's not quite thirty miles from here, I believe."

"Please, Elisha," Mother urged, "send me the information as soon as you return to Milwaukee."

"My pleasure, Charlotte," Uncle Elisha said. "That, and anything else you need."

Caroline met Martha's eyes across the table, and she knew from the smile that was brightening her sister's face that Martha had been listening too.

"Did you hear that, Caroline?" Martha whispered. "Uncle Elisha may help us find some land, and only thirty miles away! That's just a couple days away, by wagon, I think!"

"It's still too far," Caroline whispered back.

"It's much closer than out west," Martha said. "We could still come back and visit Brookfield even!"

"I don't want to go!" Caroline shot back. "I don't want to leave home!"

"Martha?" Mother called from across the room. "Come get the milk and begin filling the glasses, please."

"Yes, ma'am." Martha hurried off without another word.

"Why such a sad face?" Grandma asked as she came up beside Caroline and placed a small crock of butter in the center of the table.

Looking up into Grandma's kind eyes, Caroline felt all her Christmas happiness melting away. "Oh, Grandma," she said softly, holding back tears, "I don't want to leave our house, I don't want to leave Anna and Elsa, Mr. Ben and the schoolhouse, the barn and the church. . . ."

Grandma pulled Caroline close against her, gently stroking her hair. "You must never be afraid to journey to new places, Caroline," she said. "Just think, had Mother stayed in Boston, she would never have met your father. Change is good for the soul and good for the heart. And in every new place, we meet new friends and have new experiences, without ever losing those we left behind. Do you understand?"

"I think so."

The family soon gathered around the table to eat and exchange tale after tale of Christmases past. Caroline remained quiet, considering Grandma's wise words. It would be awful to leave Anna and Mr. Ben, and all the familiar faces, places, and sights in this town she had called home for as long as she could remember. And yet somewhere there were new friends just waiting to be met. The thought brightened her spirits.

Once the dishes were washed, dried, and put away, the family gathered in front of the hot, cheery fire. Uncle Elisha played jubilantly on his harmonica, tapping his foot and tilting his head back and forth. The children clapped and swung from arm to arm, dancing and twirling and bumping into each other until the fire lost some of its bounce and the world outside the windowpanes grew dark and settled down for the night.

"We must soon be off to bed," Uncle Elisha announced, "if Santeclaus is to have any time to visit us before daybreak."

"Who?" Eliza asked, stifling a yawn.

"Who?" Uncle Elisha repeated in surprise. "You mean to say that you've never heard of Santeclaus?"

"No, sir," a chorus of voices answered.

"Well then, I must tell you about old Santeclaus!" he said in his deep, gentle voice, dropping his harmonica into his pocket as Caroline and her sisters and brothers gathered around. "The tale goes something like this," he began.

"Old Santeclaus with much delight
His reindeer drives this frosty night

338

O'er chimney tops and tracks of snow
To bring his yearly gifts to you.

"The steady friend of virtuous youth,
The friend of duty and of truth,
Each Christmas Eve he joys to come
Where love and peace have made their
* home."*

"Is he a real person?" Caroline breathed.

"I believe so," Uncle Elisha said. "In fact, just last week I received a drawing of Santeclaus from a printer friend of mine in New York City."

"What does Sant-e-claus look like?" Henry asked, speaking the strange name slowly.

"Well, he's a plump, bearded fellow who wears a long red cape that's lined with white fur, and he carries an enormous sack on his back that's overflowing with presents." Uncle Elisha tapped his chin as he tried to remember more. "Ah, yes," he added, "in this painting I saw, the old man is standing beside a chimney with one finger on the side of his nose. And beside him on the mantel hangs a whole row of stockings, every one of them stuffed with gifts."

"Where did all the presents come from?" Martha asked.

"Why, from Santeclaus, of course," Uncle Elisha said. "Now, I think that each of us should hang a stocking on the mantel and hurry off to bed. Then Santeclaus may still have time to visit once we're asleep, and fill every one of our stockings with a Christmas surprise."

"Oh, please, Mother!" Caroline begged. "May we hang our stockings?"

"Of course," Mother agreed.

Nine empty woolen stockings soon dangled above the sputtering fire. With warm hugs and good-night wishes, William, George Henry, and John climbed into the daybed and trundle downstairs, while Caroline followed her brothers and sisters upstairs to their room, sneaking one last glance at the stockings hanging above the hearth.

The frame house was soon quiet except for the adult voices chattering and laughing down below. Long after Martha and Eliza fell off to sleep, and Henry, Joseph, and Thomas snored softly in their bed on the other side of the curtain, Caroline lay still, the cold draft in the room chilling her cheeks and fingertips as she held the heavy quilt up to her chin. Closing her eyes, she remembered every moment of this happy Christmas Eve and imagined the joyous Christmas Day that would follow. She thought about Grandma and about Uncle Elisha, who reminded her so much of her beloved father. She thought about leaving Brookfield and all her friends, but her thoughts kept turning back to the stockings hanging over the hearth, and this jolly man named Santeclaus.

Footsteps tapped softly on the stairs. Caroline turned her capped head toward the railing, and in the dim light she could barely see Mother's face. "It's bitterly cold tonight," Mother whispered. "Keep yourself tucked in."

"Yes ma'am," Caroline whispered back.

"Good night now, Caroline." She turned to go downstairs.

"Mother?" Caroline called softly into the darkness.

"Yes?" Mother turned back.

"Do you think Santeclaus will come to our house tonight?"

"Yes, I think he will."

"And will he be able to find us again if we have to leave our house and go to a new one?"

Mother climbed the last two stairs and knelt down beside the girls' bed. "Uncle Elisha told us that Santeclaus likes to come where love and peace have made their home, did he not?"

"Yes." Caroline nodded.

"Then have no doubt, Caroline," Mother said, her smile glowing in the darkness. "Santeclaus will find our home wherever we may go."

Snuggling closer to Eliza as Mother's footsteps echoed down the stairs, Caroline closed her eyes and sighed happily. She knew Grandma and Mother were right. Home wasn't a house or a town, a barn or a church, or even the kindest of friends. Home was where her sisters breathed softly in slumber beside her and her brothers rustled their straw mattress as they twisted and turned in their sleep. Home was where Mother's soft, soothing melodies floated up to the rafters. It didn't matter where they moved or settled, or what place they called home. Caroline finally understood. Home was here, in the little frame house, or anywhere she happened to live with the people she loved most.

Come Home to
Little House

The MARTHA *Years*
By Melissa Wiley
Illustrated by Renée Graef

The CHARLOTTE *Years*
By Melissa Wiley
Illustrated by Dan Andreasen

The CAROLINE *Years*
By Maria D. Wilkes
Illustrated by Dan Andreasen

The LAURA *Years*
By Laura Ingalls Wilder
Illustrated by Garth Williams

The ROSE *Years*
By Roger Lea MacBride
Illustrated by Dan Andreasen
& David Gilleece

Other LITTLE HOUSE *titles you may enjoy:*